T0128873

ZEMO

By
John Duncklee

iUniverse, Inc.
New York   Bloomington

ZEMO

This is a work of fiction. All of the characters, names, incidents, organizations, and dialogue in this novel are either the products of the author's imagination or are used fictitiously.

iUniverse books may be ordered through booksellers or by contacting:

iUniverse
1663 Liberty Drive
Bloomington, IN 47403
www.iuniverse.com
1-800-Authors (1-800-288-4677)

ISBN: 978-1-4401-1540-0 (pbk)
ISBN: 978-1-4401-1541-7 (ebk)

Printed in the United States of America

iUniverse rev. date: 12/31/2008

Life began for Zemo Doyle in a shack near the tracks because his father, Dan, worked as a section hand for the Rock Island Railroad when he wasn't drinking whiskey at the Thunderhead Saloon and Dance Hall in Vaughn, Missouri.

Dan Doyle was Irish through and through and had married an Ojibwa woman half his age named Raven of the Wind named for her shiny blue-black hair. Finding herself pregnant a few months after the wedding she began to wonder why she had married Dan. When Zemo turned six Raven of the Wind insisted that her son go to school to learn how to read and write.

By the time Zemo, his name chosen by Raven of the Wind, completed his seventeenth year he wanted to be a cowboy more than anything else in the world. His mother tried to talk him out of such ambition, but Dan was glad to see his son go about his own business so that he wouldn't have to support him any longer and he, Dan, would have more money for whiskey.

Ever since he had turned ten years-old Zemo had done day work for a couple of livestock farmers outside of town and had acquired a skill with mules, both under saddle and harness. He had ridden a lot of saddle horses also while working cattle. Zemo decided to leave Missouri and go west to become a cowboy. His other reason for leaving was to distance himself from the tirades of his drunken father.

Zemo had fond memories of his uncle who had lived as a cowboy on a ranch in Arizona for many years. The few times his Uncle Bayard had visited Missouri, Zemo knew he was quite different from his father, Dan. Finally escaping his home situation, he headed to Arizona to find his uncle, and hoped to find work on the same ranch. As soon as the bus crossed the state line between New Mexico and Arizona, Zemo grew excited at the prospect of seeing his uncle in Rinconada and finding a job cowboying at the Y Diamond Ranch. Bayard Doyle had written directions so that Zemo would find the place.

At the Rinconada bus station he bought a ticket for the twenty-mile ride north to the ranch road. Bayard had mentioned that from the main road to the ranch headquarters he would have to walk three miles. Zemo was glad he had few belongings in his carpetbag as he walked from where the driver stopped the bus for him to get off. He arrived at the Y Diamond Ranch headquarters just in time for supper, but was disappointed when his uncle told him the Y Diamond had a full crew. He was welcome to stay a while and rest up from the three-day bus ride from Missouri. Zemo rode with his uncle for two days. Once back at the corrals he asked Bayard where a good place to look for work might be.

"Well," Bayard said. "You can hang out at the Hotel Congress and ask the ranchers about work when they come into the restaurant and bar."

Just as Zemo was contemplating his return to Rinconada, the foreman came over with his forehead wrinkled. "Bayard, Jimmy Garcia got in a wreck with a wild one up in the Cañon de Los Lobos and broke his leg. Jeff drove him into town to a doctor. If your nephew wants to work, I'll put him on the payroll."

"That would suit him, wouldn't it, Zemo?"

"That would please me fine," Zemo said.

"I can give you work until Jimmy's leg mends," Jim Landers, the foreman, said.

"Fine with me," Zemo replied, through a big grin.

"All right. Bayard, why don't you and your nephew ride Cañon de Los Lobos in the morning and try to hobble that wild bastard and drag his ass back to the corrals."

"We'll do our best. Maybe with the two of us we can snag him head and heels."

"No tellin' how old the critter is. I thought we had cleaned that canyon a year ago."

"Some of those wild ones can sneak in and think they're home again," Bayard said.

The following morning after an early breakfast Zemo and Bayard saddled horses and headed for the Cañon de los Lobos. Zemo's gelding had just enough spots on his rump to be called an Appaloosa. Bayard's horse was a blood bay. They arrived at the mouth of the canyon at mid-morning.

"I'll ride up in the bottom and you ride around the north rim," Bayard said. Garcia had his wreck on the north so that old mossback might still be there. If you see the critter let me know without him seeing you and I'll find a way up to the rim."

"What does he look like?" Zemo asked.

"The boss said he was a good sized red roan with a lot of long hair on his poll between the horns. His horns are as long as those Texas cattle. He's probably one of the Quarter Circle V steers."

"What happens if he sees me before you get up on the rim?"

"Just keep an eye on him so we can go after him. I might find him on the bottom looking for water. If that's the case you'll know because you will hear me commence chasing him down."

Zemo reined his horse up the trail leading to the north rim overlooking the canyon. Bayard headed his horse up the trail at the bottom of the canyon. Zemo reached the top of the rim and looked down the steep wall of the canyon. He saw his uncle riding along the canyon floor but there was no sign of the red roan steer that had sent Garcia to the hospital. He booted his horse to follow the trail leading to the head of the canyon.

A well-used livestock and game trail entered the canyon through a small grove of juniper mixed with piñon. Zemo reined the horse down the trail hoping to meet his uncle with the news of not sighting the red roan steer. He had ridden fifty yards down the narrow trail when he saw the rear end of the red roan with its tail switching around like a whip and its head moving from side to side. The animal had stopped in its tracks, and was still trailing Garcia's braided rawhide *reata*.

Zemo reined in the horse and turned him so that he was parallel to the steer. Then he saw why the steer was acting strangely. Zemo's uncle had reached a point in the trail where he was visible to the steer.

Suddenly the red roan wheeled around and began sprinting up the trail toward Zemo, who remained wide-eyed at the hairy head and wild look in the steer's eyes. The steer shook his head and snorted. The mucous hung from his nostrils. Zemo grabbed his lariat and began to wave it as the steer approached on what seemed to Zemo a collision course. There was nowhere for Zemo to go. Just before he reached Zemo, the steer lowered his shaggy head and dove between the horse's legs, bumping his belly. The horse reared and leaped out of the way. Zemo came close to falling to the ground. He had dropped his loop midst the confusion so he quickly coiled it and put it over the saddle-horn. Bayard arrived.

"Get after that bastard," Bayard said. "You came close to having a helluva wreck."

Zemo reined the horse around and headed back up the trail. He could see the red roan ahead but he had doubts that they would be able to get close enough to toss a loop over the horns. When the two riders reached the rim of the canyon they saw the rump of the steer heading through the piñon and juniper. They rode until it was evident the red roan had put too much distance between them. Bayard reined up and

Zemo followed. The Appaloosa dropped his head to grab a mouthful of grama grass. Zemo pulled his reins and the horse continued chewing.

"That critter is full-eared and probably *orejano*," Bayard said.

"What's that Uncle Bayard?"

"*Orejano* is what the Mexicans call a maverick, a critter with no brand."

"That's probably why he is no steer," Zemo said. "That red roan devil is a bull."

"Are you sure?" Bayard asked.

"I watched him looking at you. I got the rear view of that fellow and what was hanging down had to be a bull's equipment."

"I reckon we might as well head back," Bayard said. "I found his waterhole down in the canyon. We can probably get him tomorrow unless the crafty bastard waters at night. If there were more strays we might build a trap, but it's hardly worth it for just one. Besides, from what Garcia said the damn wild devil would probably tear the trap down unless we built it out of pipe."

"That would mean packing a lot of pipe up to where you want the trap," Zemo said.

"If this was my country," Bayard said. "I'd shoot the bastard and make jerky out of him."

"How do you make jerky, Uncle Bayard?"

"You cut the meat in thin strips, trim off the fat, put salt and pepper on it and hang it on a line to dry. But you want to make sure you put plenty of pepper on. That way it's tough to tell the difference from the fly shit and the pepper," Bayard said and laughed at his own joke.

The following morning they saddled up earlier than usual and arrived at the mouth of the canyon shortly after sunrise. Bayard inspected the trail for the red roan's tracks. "If he's up the canyon, he didn't come in this way or he would have covered my tracks of yesterday. If he came down off the rim, he might be at the waterhole right now. I'll ride the rim and you can ride a ways toward the waterhole. It's about a mile up the canyon. Pull up when you see the canyon walls narrow down to about twenty feet. Wait there and if that bastard heads down toward you, do your best to keep him in the canyon."

"Suppose he acts like he did yesterday?" Zemo asked.

"You'll have more room down here and you might get a chance to toss your loop around those damned horns. I'll be riding down so he will most likely head this way since he won't see you."

Bayard took the trail Zemo had ridden the day before. Zemo walked the Appaloosa up the trail on the floor of Cañon de los Lobos until he noticed the canyon walls narrow down. As he sat on the Appaloosa, he took his lariat down and made a fairly large loop that would sail over the bull's horns if he got the chance to throw accurately. He figured it would take his uncle at least an hour to reach the head of the canyon, and another half hour to reach the waterhole.

Zemo knew that working cattle took patience as well as skill. He stood fairly confident of his skill with the lariat, but was not sure about how much patience he had waiting for his uncle to start the bull down canyon. He wanted to ride to the waterhole and start the bull up the canyon toward Bayard because he didn't want to miss a throw at the red roan devil. He had used a lariat many times doing day work back in Missouri, but he had never encountered an animal as wild as the red roan bull. He thought back to the day before when he had told his uncle about the red roan being a bull and not a steer and grinned.

The sun climbed. The canyon lit up. Zemo sat still in the saddle. The Appaloosa relaxed. Every so often Zemo nudged the gelding so that he would be ready to plunge after the bull should the wild one charge down canyon toward them. He wondered about his father and mother. He had not been surprised that his uncle had the same black hair and ruddy complexion as his father. He also wondered if Uncle Bayard went to town and got as drunk as Dan Doyle.

Thankfully, the sun cast its shadow so that where Zemo waited stood in the shade. There were a few trees, mostly sycamore and ash, in the canyon below where Zemo waited for the red roan bull.

Finally he heard the thumping of hooves up canyon. Zemo nudged the Appaloosa and kept his eyes on the trail to be ready for the maverick red roan bull. The sound of the hooves beating the floor of the canyon grew louder. At a point where the trail skirted a sycamore that was beginning to sprout out its spring leaves, he saw the bull heading his way at a fast trot with his head high and tossing from side to side. Zemo booted the Appaloosa up the trail toward the bull. The bull slid to a stop, focused on Zemo and the Appaloosa, shook his head and snorted. He pawed the ground with his right hoof and then with the left. As the bull shifted back and forth, Zemo saw that he seemed to be trying to make up his mind which direction to go. For a moment, Zemo admired the red roan. What a valiant wild one trying to stay free!

Taking advantage of the bull's confusion, Bayard spurred the blood bay toward the bull, circling his loop, waiting for the right chance to toss. The lariat whined as it went toward the bull's head and then wrapped around the ringed horns, denoting an aging animal. Zemo saw what had happened and quickly spurred the Appaloosa toward the bull. Bayard kept the bull at bay, and Zemo got behind the wild one and threw his loop at the bull's hind legs. Instantly Zemo saw that he had made a perfect toss, and jerked the lariat so that the bull's hind legs got caught. Zemo reined the Appaloosa away to tighten the lariat. Bayard had his blood bay stretching his lariat. The bull fell. Bayard swiftly dismounted and tied a pigging string around the bull's hind legs.

"Zemo, get down here and get this bastard's front legs hobbled, and we'll put our lariats around those horns and lead him back to headquarters. We'll brand the bastard and give Jimmy Garcia back his *reata*."

Zemo dismounted and hobbled the bull's front legs just tight enough to slow him down, and loose enough so that they could encourage him to make his way back to the ranch headquarters. When they took the pigging string off the hind legs, the bull rose, shook his scraggly head and Zemo and Bayard, with both their lariats around the bull's horns, led their prey back to the ranch headquarters without further mishap.

It was close to evening when they got the red roan bull corralled at headquarters. Jim Landers ambled out from the cook shack. "Keep those hobbles on that wild one or he might bust through the corrals," he said. "We will brand him tomorrow. I assume he's a maverick."

"Yeah, he's a maverick all right, and he's also a bull, Bayard replied.

"We'll take care of that when we have him down."

"If you're going to haul him in to the auction, a steer that old and a bull will bring about the same," Bayard said.

"You're probably right, Bayard. Keep his manhood intact," Landers said."

Zemo realized that his uncle knew what he was talking about. He carried Jimmy Garcia's rawhide *reata* into the bunkhouse. Jimmy had come home and sat in the one stuffed chair in the bunkhouse. Zemo walked over and handed him the *reata*.

"I never thought I would see that again," Jimmy said. "Gracias."

"That red roan is a terror," Zemo said.

"He sure is. I had the *reata* snug around his horns and then he turned and charged my horse and me. When the steer hit my horse he fell on me and that's when my leg snapped. I had a hard time getting back aboard because my leg hurt worse than anything I have ever known."

The following day Landers sent Bayard and Zemo out to the far south end of the ranch to check on strays.

The foreman told Bayard that he had seen a cow and calf at the southern most water hole. First, however, they saddled up and branded the red roan bull; then put him a small corral near the loading chute.

As they rode south Bayard looked over at his nephew. "You did a helluva good job yesterday, Zemo. I believe you'll make a hand."

Zemo smiled. "That's what I came out here for," he said.

"Too bad we have a full crew. At least it will be a month or so before Jimmy can ride again. We probably won't get a chance at another *orejano* bull, but there might be some excitement."

"When is the gather?" Zemo asked.

"We ship in October or November depending on the summer rains. They were good this year. As you can see, the grass is high and looks strong. So, probably, November we'll ship. That means we will start gatherin' slowly in the middle of October. We'll brand any new calves we might have missed last spring and ship all the weaners. The boss likes to wean early so the calves don't stand around shrinking as they bawl for their mamas."

"I wish I could stay for the gather," Zemo said.

"I'll speak to Jim Landers for you. You can damn sure handle a horse and you are really good with that lariat."

"Thanks Uncle Bayard."

"I gotta tell you, Zemo. You're a helluva lot different than my brother. I got a tad spooked when I read your letter that you were heading my way, but after yesterday I am sure glad you showed up. It has been fun getting to know the nephew I haven't seen since you were eight years old. Don't ever let that whiskey get to you like it did brother Dan."

"I've never tasted it," Zemo said. "I expect some day I'll give it a try. I am glad I came out here, Uncle Bayard. I have always wondered what you were really like. My father has said over and over that you chose to be a goddam cowboy and wouldn't make enough to cover your liquor bill."

"I don't have a liquor bill to pay," Bayard said. "By dab, there's that stray cow and calf over under that mesquite tree. I know damn well she ain't wearin' our brand cause her ear mark is two swallow forks and our's is an under bit on the left ear with a crop on the right."

"Do you know who owns her?" Zemo asked

"Hell yes. They must have put that old gal in here to get a decent bull. Our neighbors to the south have a bailing wire outfit and they don't have enough bulls to cover their cowherd. Their cows enjoy a free lunch besides. We know what is going on so we check the country regularly."

"I used to look for strays back in Missouri. One farmer had a saddle mule that could just about sense that there was a stray in the pasture. Of course, the pastures weren't as big as they are out here."

"Let's get that old Nellie to her feet and drive her south to the fence-line," Bayard said. "There's a gate about a mile from here. We'll be driving her toward water rather than away from it. Cattle drive easier toward water. When you start the devils from water they are inclined to cut back. I expect that's cause they don't want to end up thirsty."

They got the cow and calf moving south to the fence marking the border between the ranches. "Zemo, ride on ahead until you come to a gate. Open it and then ride on past so this old gal doesn't decide to keep going beyond the opening."

Zemo rode ahead, found the gate and opened it. He remounted, rode twenty yards further along the fence and a short distance away from it, stopped and waited for the pair to arrive. The cow and calf knew where they were going and ambled to the other side of the fence. Bayard dismounted and closed the gate. Once remounted, he turned to Zemo.

"Running cows out in this country is tough as hell. If it don't come a drought, the price of beef goes to hell," he said. "One reason I work for wages is that I haven't saved enough money to have a cushion."

"What do you mean, Uncle Bayard?"

"I could probably beg, borrow and steal enough to get started on a bunch of cows, but if a drought happened by, I wouldn't have enough to carry the operation through until it rained again."

"I want to get a ranch going someday," Zemo said.

"From what little I know of you, you probably will. Just make sure you have a cushion."

Zemo thought about what his uncle had said. He had no idea what it would cost to get a bunch of cows and a place to graze them. Neither did he have a notion how he would earn enough money to make a start. Then, he had an idea.

"Uncle Bayard, have you ever entered a rodeo?"

"Just once," Bayard said. "I rode a Brahma bull for about two seconds and lost my ten dollar entry fee. That was enough for me cause I was only making sixty a month and found."

"I was thinking I might be able to win enough in a rodeo to get me a ranch and some cows."

"Zemo, there's a thousand rodeo hands that once thought that and there's probably three in the history of rodeo that has made enough to buy a hundred head of mother cows, but where in hell would they graze 'em?"

"I can rope pretty well, and I can sure stay on bucking horses. If I can ride a bucking mule to a stand-still I ought to be able to stay aboard a rodeo bronc for ten seconds."

"Just by the way you're talkin' I can tell that you are aimin' to try your hand at rodeo. Remember this as long as you won't listen to the else I have to say; you'll never win enough ridin' broncs in rodeos to pay your expenses unless you make the big shows like San Francsico, Tucson or Calgary. The small town rodeos can't afford to pay big prize money."

They rode back to headquarters, Zemo mulling over in his mind what his uncle had said. It took quite a spell before Zemo thought he had it all figured out.

"Uncle Bayard got farted off that bull and figures he could never ride another past ten seconds so he quit," Zemo thought. "Since then he has worked for wages and hasn't a prayer of getting a ranch together. Hell's fire, let Uncle Bayard work for wages. Maybe someday I'll hire him on to ride for me."

Zemo rode with his uncle every day, looking for strays, branding the *orejanos*, and generally checking the cattle. They never encountered the likes of the roan bull again. Zemo wondered if that old bull had escaped from the past or had appeared just to challenge him. As his uncle had said those longhorn cattle were definitely a thing of the past. So he wondered why that wild longhorn bull had wandered into the Y Diamond Ranch country. One day he asked his uncle about his question.

"Zemo, there's a feller owns the Quarter Circle V outfit close to Cimmaron. He came here from back east a while ago with a bunch of money and bought that ranch. He's from somewhere where they deal in money. This feller decides he is going to bring back the Texas Longhorns so they don't become extinct. That's the way he put it at a meeting of the cattlemen's association."

"What's wrong with that?" Zemo asked.

"There's nothing wrong with buying the ranch or putting Texas Longhorns to graze it. However, this feller figured he didn't need to brand his calves because he was the only one grazing longhorn cattle. That roan bull we took to town was probably one of his first calves because it was a maverick."

"He's no maverick anymore since we branded it," Zemo said.

"You got that right, Nephew. The boss, Sam Haskell, figured he didn't want any longhorn calves from our cows, but come spring there might be some if Roany found any of our cows to make love to."

"That roan might have torn out some fence in his travels," Zemo said.

"I imagine he did. I hate riding fence lines. Maybe the boss will find someone else if he thinks about it long enough. Fences are more worry than they're worth."

"What do you mean, Uncle Bayard? We would have to chase all over to find our cattle."

"That's the way it used to be. When they started to use barbed wire, the range was doomed," Bayard said. The buffalo migrated with the seasons and didn't concentrate on any one piece of country. Then cattle arrived and did the same. But after fences got here the cattle could no longer migrate like the buffalo did so the country got overgrazed. Then, of course, there's some cowmen who get greedy and think they can put more cattle on the country than it will carry."

"I have heard tell about that," Zemo said.

Payday came and Zemo looked at the check. He had not discussed wages with the foreman so the hundred-dollar check made him feel like a top hand. Bayard stayed at the bunkhouse, but Zemo and Garcia went to town with one of the other cowboys who owned an old model "A" Ford. The other cowboy was a man from Wyoming who hoped to spend the winter in the warm part of Arizona. Frank Spencer always went to town on paydays because Frank Spencer liked to frequent the bars and try to find women. Frank was old enough to know that the only women he would find in the bars he visited in Rinconada would cost money. Frank had been doing that sort of courting most of his life. His experience with women, that is, the kind of women he met in the bars where he drank, had convinced Frank that he should stay single. His logic led him to believe that since the women he met in the bars were professional lovers, he would be better off single so he could enjoy the variety he had become accustomed to. After dropping Garcia off at his parents' house for a week's stay, Frank drove to The Silver Dollar, parked the car a block away from the saloon, stuffed the ignition keys into the front right hand pocket of his Levis, and led the way to the entrance.

Zemo followed. As they reached the front door of the Silver Dollar, Frank turned and pointed toward the entrance. "Here's the best place in town," he said. "Come on in and have a drink."

"I don't think I am old enough," Zemo said.

"Aw hell," Frank said. "If anyone asks you how old you are, just tell 'em you've had the seven-year-itch three times."

Zemo had no idea what the seven-year-itch was and figured it must be something he had heard about body lice, but still had no clue how long an infestation lasted. He followed Frank through the entrance.

Zemo had seen the interior of bars from time to time when he had gone in search of is father back in Missouri. But, when he walked into the Silver Dollar he had a feeling that he did not belong there. He wanted to flee the noise, the smell and the atmosphere of the saloon. He knew Frank would insist on drinking and he knew he would have a drink with Frank. Underneath he feared that he might end up like his father.

There were several customers standing up to the bar, back of which a barkeep with sandy colored hair wearing a white shirt and black bow tie hustled around taking orders and making drinks. The bottles were arranged in front of an ornate wood framed mirror. An empty space separated the bar from the lounge. There were a few customers sitting at some tables that filled a room that looked to be thirty by forty feet. In one corner there were six men seated at a round table playing cards.

Frank led Zemo to a small table by the west wall, told him to sit down and be patient while he went to the bar to order their drinks. "I assume you drink tequila," Frank said.

Zemo said nothing nor gestured in any way. He didn't know tequila from coffee. Frank walked to the bar, ordered, cashed his paycheck then returned to sit with Zemo. The waitress, a comely brunette with a dress that showed her canyon-like cleavage brought a bottle of tequila and two shot-glasses with a small plate containing lime quarters and a salt shaker.

"Thanks Lucy," Frank said. "Are you busy after work?"

"It depends," the woman said.

"On what?" Frank asked.

"Hell's fire, Frank, you should know by now that you have to pay in advance."

Frank reached into his pocket, withdrew a twenty-dollar bill and handed it to Lucy. She took the bill demurely and stuffed it into her brassiere. What money she made after hours was hers, not the Silver Dollar's.

"I'll let you know when I am ready to close out here. You know where my room is."

Lucy left the table to wait on other customers. Frank poured tequila into the shot glasses and handed one to his companion. "Let's have a drink to Lucy," he said. "She is one fine woman."

Frank lifted his glass to toast Lucy who had gone about her business. Zemo sat rigid in his chair.

"Well, Zemo. Are you gonna toast Lucy? Frank asked.

"I don't know what you are talking about," Zemo said. "This is the first drink I ever had in front of me."

"Well Sonny," Frank said. "Lick your wrist and shake some salt on it. Then, lick it off your wrist. After that toss that shot of tequila down your throat, and suck on the lime."

Zemo followed Frank's directions. The tequila felt like liquid fire as it plunged down his esophagus. He almost coughed to throw it out, but managed to maintain his composure.

"Not too shabby, eh?" Frank said." Let's have another."

Frank poured out two more shots and the two cowboys tossed down the second shot. By the time they had had three shots Frank leaned over toward Zemo. "Big Joe Goodman just came in," Frank said.

"Who is Big Joe Goodman?" Zemo asked.

"He's the neighbor who runs Texas Longhorns," Frank said, still leaning toward Zemo. "He don't cotton to anyone from our outfit because he knows we have branded some of his strays."

"He looks like he has been drinking somewhere besides here," Zemo said. "What is he doing with Lucy?"

"He's probably trying to make a date with her after she closes, but I've already taken care of that."

They watched as Lucy pointed over to their table and Big Joe headed their way. He stopped three feet from their table. "Lucy says you paid her in advance," Big Joe said in an accent that betrayed his origins in New York City. "I'll pay you the twenty plus another fifty to take your place."

"You haven't got enough money to buy me out, Goodman," Frank said. "Lucy and I go back a long way."

"How is it that you know my name?"

"I work for your neighbor, the Y Diamond."

"Are you one of those guilty of branding my Texas Longhorns with your brand?"

"When those devils tear out the fence to get to our cows, you can depend that we will brand the mavericks and send them to the auction. You can always go down there on Saturdays and buy 'em back."

"You should know those cattle are mine because nobody else raises Texas Longhorns around here."

"If you branded them we would drive them back into your country. Goodman, you really don't know what you're doing. A maverick is fair game no matter how long the bastard's horns are."

"Well, I suppose that I will offer Lucy a hundred dollars and you will be out of luck and out your twenty," Goodman said, then turned on his heel and strode to the bar.

Zemo kept his eyes focused on Big Joe Goodman because something in the tone of Goodman's voice made the hair on the back of Zemo's neck rise and wave around in his mind. He watched Goodman take out a hundred dollar bill and hand it to Lucy. They were too far away for Zemo to hear their conversation, but he saw Lucy push Goodman's hand that held the bill back toward him. She spun around and headed to the far end of the bar.

Goodman shoved his money into his trouser pocket, turned a bit unsteadily and began walking back to Frank and Zemo's table. Zemo saw him clench his fists. Without a word to Frank, Zemo jumped up from his chair, plunged at Goodman with his head lowered and aimed at Goodman's stomach. Zemo hit the larger man so hard that Goodman fell backwards and slammed his head on the floor. Zemo cocked his right arm with fist made, but saw that Goodman remained unconscious on the floor.

Frank stood up with an amazed look on his face. Several customers from the bar stepped over. Not knowing if they were friends of Goodman or not, Zemo returned to the table. One of the men followed him and held out his hand. "I don't know who you are," he said. "But you did a fine job on that sorry bastard. He came out here with his bundle of money and thinks he can rule the country like he did in New York."

Zemo turned away from the man as the bartender approached. "I think you and Frank ought to make yourselves scarce," the barkeep said. "I don't want any more trouble here."

By this time Frank had returned and had grabbed the bottle of tequila. "Zemo, let's get going."

The two cowboys from the Y Diamond walked away from the saloon. Once back in the Model A, Frank uncorked the bottle and offered it to his friend. Zemo tipped the bottle and took a long pull on it. "I don't know why, but all of a sudden I lost control and went after that idiot," Zemo said.

After taking his turn at the bottle, Frank patted Zemo's arm. "You did the right thing. I saw him clench his fists and I was getting ready to meet him only you beat me to the punch. Where did you learn to use your head as a battering ram?"

"I never did that before. I have never been in a fight either. I have only watched bulls go after one another. I don't even remember thinking about what I did before I did it."

"How about another snort?" Frank asked.

"I suppose one more wouldn't make me drunker than I already am."

"I'll keep an eye on the Silver Dollar to make sure I see Lucy when she leaves. You can wait here in the car and we will get back to the ranch and get some sleep."

A half hour went by until Lucy left The Silver Dollar. Frank opened the door, stepped out on the street and followed her to her apartment two blocks away. Meanwhile Zemo finished the tequila and went to sleep lying on the seat of the car. Later, Frank returned from his pleasure with Lucy, awakened Zemo and they headed back to the Y Diamond.

Bayard stopped by Zemo's bunk on his way to breakfast. "Better get up, Nephew. That breakfast might get cold."

Zemo opened his eyes and looked up at his uncle. "I think I'll pass up breakfast this morning, Uncle Bayard."

"What did you do, spend your pay check on whiskey?"

"I didn't cash my pay check," Zemo replied.

"You must have had a snoot full if you don't hanker for breakfast," Bayard said, and left the bunkhouse.

Zemo rose up enough to see a lump under the blankets in Frank Spencer's bed. Then he pulled the covers over his head and went back to sleep until Bayard returned from breakfast and rousted him out to go to the barn and saddle his horse for a day's work.

Bayard Doyle waited until Zemo had his horse saddled before he told his nephew that they were to ride fence along the boundary between the Quarter Circle V and the Y Diamond to try and find the hole in the fence where the roan bull entered. Since there were two of them Bayard decided to have a pack mule to carry wire and tools to fix whatever they found. "There's no use looking for and finding the break unless we have the where-with-all to fix it," he said. "Catch up that pack mule and saddle him. I'll get the tools together," Bayard said.

"I remember you telling me you didn't like riding fence lines, Uncle Bayard."

"I don't, but it has to be done and we have been elected to find that break by none other than Jim Landers."

Zemo felt his head throb. He wished he had never tasted the tequila. He also wished he had never gone to town with Frank Spencer. By the time the sun said it was noonday Zemo wanted most of all to ride back to the bunkhouse and crawl into his bunk.

Bayard spotted the hole in the fence line where it crossed a water gap, a place where there was an arroyo. "I didn't see any wire cuts on that roan bull, but he sure took this water gap out in fine fashion," Bayard said. "It looks like we need to replace most of the wire."

"I'll get the pack mule unloaded," Zemo said, anxious to get the work finished and get back to headquarters.

They cut away the twisted mess that the bull had caused and strung new wire, replacing the hangers on the bottom strand. The hangers were nothing more than fence posts tied to the bottom strand so they would float when water ran in the arroyo. Once the drainage cleared the hangers would return to hold the wire low to discourage cattle from squeezing underneath. The red roan bull had not been discouraged.

Back at headquarters Zemo hurried to take care of his horse and the pack mule. His headache had diminished somewhat, but he had a great desire to close his eyes for the hour before suppertime. As he finished the chores he started to leave the barn for the bunkhouse. Bayard stood in the barnyard.

"I didn't think you'd make it by the way you looked this morning. I might remind you that your father, my brother, probably feels that way damn near every morning of his life."

"He doesn't drink tequila," Zemo said, and headed for the bunkhouse without further conversation with his uncle.

A week later Jimmy Garcia's relatives drove him to the ranch. Jimmy found Landers getting into the ranch pickup and told him that his father had taken sick and he would have to quit the ranch job. He packed his belongings and left the Y Diamond in his cousin's Chevy pickup truck.

Upon his return from riding for strays and checking for open gates, Zemo's eyes lit up when Landers told him he had a permanent job if he wanted to stay on. When he told his uncle the good news, Bayard shook his hand and congratulated him.

"This is better than rodeo," Bayard said.

"I haven't given up on that idea," Zemo replied. "At a hundred a month I never will make enough to get a ranch started."

"That might be, but at least you will get a hundred a month and found which is a helluva lot more than you can count on from rodeo."

* * *

The spring weeds poked out of the ground and the cattle seemed to run around nipping off as many morsels as they could before going in to their customary waterholes. Cows slicked off and their flanks filled in spite of nursing calves.

Jim Landers stopped by the bunkhouse one evening to tell the men that he planned to start the spring gather in two weeks. "Have you fellows seen many dry cows out there?"

"There's a couple that water at Horseshoe Tank and another over at Slocum's," Bayard said.

"I saw two dry cows at Hallorhan Tank but I think most of the cows around Hall Tank have calves," Zemo said.

"What I have seen in my travels, I think we have a damn good calf crop this year," Landers said. "I told Mister Haskell about the gather and he said he would saddle up for it and give us an extra hand. He's a good hand and we can always use more help, especially at the spring gather when we brand more calves than in the fall."

After Landers left the bunkhouse Zemo quizzed his uncle. "I thought you called it a roundup," he said.

"That's movie talk and the way those writers who think they know the West write their novels. I doubt many of those jaspers ever rode a gather," Bayard said. "I read one story that the famous author had a horse go a hundred miles in two hours."

"Even I know that's impossible," Zemo said.

"Just show me a horse that can run that fast and I'll buy that cayuse and go into the race horse business on borrowed money," Bayard said.

"How come that stuff gets written?"

"Beats me," Bayard said scratching his head. "I expect it all comes out of New York and they don't know any more than their writers. I got tired of that kind of reading and these days I only read stuff that isn't fiction. I like history, especially about the Apache. They were quite a bunch of people."

"I don't read a lot," Zemo said. "I can read pretty fast, but I never seem to take time to sit down and do it."

"Well, now that you found steady work you might try finding out what you like to read and pick up some books in town on payday instead of an aching head and a disrupted gut."

"Where do I find these books?"

"Well, there's a used bookstore on Second Avenue. You can spend days in there. The books are not expensive. If you go to the library you can check out books for free, but you have to get them back in two weeks."

"I can easily read a book in two weeks," Zemo said.

"But, likely you won't get to town more than once a month."

"Next payday I will look into all this. I like to read, and like you say, Uncle Bayard, it will give me something to do evenings. I've noticed you opening a book after supper."

"It costs a lot less than getting drunk and I never get a headache from it."

Zemo didn't get a chance to go to town before the spring gather began. Jim Landers took charge of the gather even though Sam Haskell, the owner, rode with them.

Sam had lived an exciting life. He had returned from being a navy carrier pilot during World War II to marry a woman, who would eventually inherit an airline and a company that was one of the first to amass enough farmland to start an agribusiness. Sam loved Irene Haskell and couldn't have cared less about her potential wealth. He had a nest egg of his own that he had managed to parlay into enough capital gains to buy the Y Diamond and a restaurant specializing in beef without hormones. Part of the Y Diamond operation consisted of a modified feedlot where the steers and heifers ate more alfalfa hay than they did grain. Those cattle, when dressed out, were the steaks and roasts offered by Sam's restaurant. The amount and cuts not used went to a wholesale meat company that Sam wanted to buy. However, he didn't want to ask for money from Irene. By the time Zemo went to work for the Y Diamond, Sam figured he had another three years to operate his cattle and restaurant businesses before he could come up with the numbers he needed to convince his banker that he could handle buying the wholesale meat outlet.

A week before the gather began, Landers got word to all the neighbors about the impending operation so they could join to help and take any of their strays home. This is common range courtesy. Cowmen who don't inform their neighbors of a gather are more often than not held suspect to branding someone else's calf or calves.

The gather began in the early morning hours with everyone riding to the far northern end of the Y Diamond and making a sweep south to a waterhole a mile and a half from the northern border. Zemo had ridden out the morning before and closed the gate on the water lot, a corral that enclosed the big *represo*, an earthen dam that held water year round most years except during a prolonged drought. Most of the cattle that grazed that area would be waiting at the gate for water.

When the riders had driven the rest of the bovine from the surrounding area to join those waiting at the closed gate, one of the riders would close the gate and all the cattle were corralled. The sweep was necessary because a lot of the mother cows left their calves with what some people might call a "baby sitter cow" that kept watch over the young of several nursing cows. Once the mothers returned the baby sitter made her way to water and left her calf for her friends to watch over.

The sweep gathered all the cattle in the area; cows, calves and bulls. Once the men had the cattle in the water lot they began preparing for branding, earmarking, castrating, dehorning and vaccinating the calves against Blackleg, Brucellosis and Malignant edema, three bovine diseases that can be virulent.

Landers rode into the bunch of calves and roped them. Zemo flanked them to the ground and tied their legs to keep them down. Bayard did the branding; Zemo cut the earmarks; Sam Haskell took charge of the vaccinations, and Landers castrated the bull calves. One neighbor had showed up and was given the job of keeping the branding fire going as well as keeping the syringes full of vaccine. Big Joe Goodman did not show up, nor did he send a representative.

Irene Haskell arrived at noon driving a pickup truck carrying food and coffee. The men stopped work only after the last calf got turned loose to go find its mother. In the meantime Irene put the coffee pot on the branding fire along with the big pot of beef stew she had made for the men. She had a bale of hay in the back of the pickup that Zemo carried out to where the horses stood in the water lot. He broke it open and put flakes of alfalfa hay around so the horses could fill their bellies while the men fill theirs. Jim Landers opened the gate and Bayard got the cattle moving through and out. Mother cows bawled for their calves and the calves, somewhat in shock from the entire episode, bawled for their mothers.

Bayard sat next to Zemo as they ate their dinner. "Cows and calves will each go to the last place they nursed. That's the way they mother-up," Bayard said. "From when we separated the calves from their mothers in the water lot they had no chance to nurse. Therefore they will head out to that last place where they were together."

"Hmm," said Zemo.

After Irene left with the dirty pots and dishes, Landers took the bull calves' testicles out of a small bucket and put them on the coals of the fire to roast. "Oysters anyone?" Landers asked when the delicacy was ready to savor. The men crowded around the boss and helped themselves.

The noon meal finished, and after a two-hour ride the men returned to headquarters. Landers had sent Zemo to close the gate on the water lot named "Walker" It had been named after the man who had homesteaded that section under the Desert Homestead Act. Six hundred forty acres wasn't enough land from which to make a living from desert country, so he had moved on after selling out to the man who was putting together what became the Y Diamond Ranch.

Zemo arrived in plenty of time for supper. He unsaddled his horse and made sure there was plenty of grain in the *morral*, a bag that hung from the horse's neck. All the horse had to do was lower its head to the ground and grab the grain with its mouth. When his horse finished the grain, Zemo removed the *morral*, and let his horse battle for the hay in the mangers that were in the middle of the corral.

The Walker section at the foot of the mountain range always proved to be the most difficult part of the Y Diamond to gather because there were intermittent streams on the slopes of the mountains so that shutting the water lot gate would not necessarily result in all the cattle waiting outside it in the morning. Therefore, after finishing with what cattle were there the following morning, the crew rode up the mountain slope to an old line camp that had a small set of corrals and a cabin where the men could sleep. This arrangement made it possible to get an early start to gather the cattle that ranged in the mountains. That sweep would last most of the morning and into the afternoon, according to Bayard.

Irene had driven the pickup to the line camp and left provisions for a late dinner, supper and breakfast. Bayard would be the camp cook in addition to his riding duties. Zemo helped his uncle by cleaning the dishes and pots and pans after the meals.

As usual, after supper the crew sat around the table with their coffee. Sam Haskell, a man of average height with an athletic build ran his fingers through his graying hair that had never diminished in density. The men were silent because they could see that the Y Diamond owner had something on his mind.

"I wouldn't be here today if it hadn't been for an Australian radio operator on an island in the south Pacific during World War II," he said.

"Why is that?" Zemo asked.

"I flew off the Wasp, one of our aircraft carriers. One morning we attacked a Japanese flotilla that included a battleship, two cruisers and several destroyers, I don't remember how many. At any rate, we had been following them for several days. We launched our aircraft at dawn. I was fourth to take off flying a Grumman Avenger, a damn fine single engine torpedo bomber. I had a machine gunner behind, and once we were airborne I checked with him about any enemy aircraft in the vicinity. He told me that he couldn't see any and that the sky looked all clear. When all aircraft had taken off we rendezvoused and flew into two formations, the Wildcat fighters above and the Avengers below."

"Why that way?" Bayard asked.

"The fighters flew cover for us so that if any enemy aircraft appeared, we could concentrate on our mission to try to sink as many of the enemy ships as we could."

"Do you mean you had to depend completely on the fighters to protect you as you went in on the attack? Jim Landers asked.

"That's about it except we had our machine gunners protecting our port and starboard sides and, of course, aft."

"That sounds kind of scary," Zemo said.

"Damn straight it was scary," Haskell said. "The whole damn war was scary. I doubt if war is ever fun except when you're ashore on liberty. But, we never saw that for over a year."

"Did you find the Japanese ships?" Zemo asked.

"We flew in on a vector run that had them all on target," Haskell said, rubbing his nose a little. "We knew the moment we sighted the flotilla that we were taking them by surprise. My Avenger squadron swooped down and flew toward our targets. Mine was a destroyer that I was supposed to sink with one fish. I dropped that torpedo at perfect distance so that the captain of that tin can would never be able to dodge. Once I let that fish go I climbed as quickly as that Avenger would go to avoid the machine gun and anti-aircraft fire from the ship. I had to watch for our aircraft so as not to crash into any that were coming out of their torpedo runs. My entire focus became to watch for my squadron mates."

"How many Japanese ships did your squadron sink?" Zemo asked.

"Hold on, I need to tell you what else happened," Haskell said. "I had just reached altitude for the run home when I saw a Japanese Zero fighter aircraft heading my way all hell bent for election. I knew he had me in his sights and was just waiting to get in closer. I peeled off and dove in a tailspin to try to throw him off. But those Zeros were fast and could turn on a dime. My evasive action didn't get me out of the predicament. I heard our machine gun firing steadily then the noise stopped. I saw the tracers from the Zero ripping my fuselage and clicked on the intercom to see how my machine gunner had come through. There was no answer. I could feel the grimace invade my face."

"Was the machine gunner killed?" Zemo asked.

"I didn't know for sure. The Zero came back and again I tried evasive action again hoping that our Wildcats would show up and get the bastard off my tail. Just as I spotted two of our fighters homing in on the Zero, my aircraft began behaving badly and I found it difficult to maintain altitude. I knew I was going down."

"Did the Wildcats get the Zero?" Zemo asked.

"They got him all right. I saw smoke coming out of his tail as he plunged toward the sea. I spotted an island with a nice calm looking bay as I headed down. I knew I could crash land there if only I could keep airborne long enough to reach it. I looked out and saw that one of my problems was that the starboard wing tip had been shot away. I looked at the tail section through the rear view and saw that I had only half a rudder. I must have had a guardian angel looking after me that day because I made it to the bay, opened the canopy and sat her down beautifully."

"What is the canopy?" Landers asked.

"It is the Plexiglas window that covers the cockpit while you're flying," Haskell explained. "I climbed out the seat as quickly as possible because I knew I had little time before the damn thing sank. First I went to the window aft and saw that my machine gunner was dead. His entire face had been blown away. I vomited. Next I released the life raft and tried to get the machine gunner's body out before the aircraft sank. All of a sudden, though, it took the gunner to a watery grave. I inflated the raft, climbed aboard and began paddling three hundred yards to shore."

"What happened to the machine gunner's body?" Zemo asked.

"As far as I know it is still inside the Avenger at the bottom of that bay. I reported it all when I got back but I have no idea what happened. You lose track of things during war. At any rate just as I was about to get out of the raft and pull it up onto the beach a man came toward me smiling.

"Nice landin' there mate," he said. "I'm Australian. The blokes have me camped here with a radio to report ship movements. Name's Freddy."

"I am really glad to see you, Freddy," I said. "I'm Sam Haskell."

"Freddy said he was sure glad to have another human being to talk to. He told me that an entire regiment of Japanese soldiers occupied the other end of the island but they never seemed inquisitive enough to explore his end. He had me deflate the raft and hide it under a pile of palm leaves. Then we walked a ways to his camp that had a view of the shipping lanes out to sea. He showed me his radio, then turned it on to call and report that I had shown up and needed retrieving."

"They will get in touch with your navy and they will probably send a submarine out to pick you up," Freddy said.

"How long did you stay with Freddy," Zemo asked.

"It was pretty close to two weeks. One night Freddy told me to go down and inflate the raft. It was dark. The bay was calm and smooth as glass. Freddy stayed by the radio to get any message from the submarine. Suddenly he was by my side telling me that the sub would arrive at any minute and would signal with three blinks of a light toward shore. I was then to get in the raft and paddle out to the submarine. We said our good byes when the sub surfaced and I got into the raft. I saw the signal and paddled out to my rescuers."

"Have you ever seen Freddy since the war?" Landers asked.

"Never saw Freddy again but I have sure thought about him a way out there with all those Japanese soldiers on the other end of that island."

"What happened to you when the war was over?" Landers asked.

"I went back to Colorado and married Irene."

"Didn't you want to keep flying for the Navy?" Zemo asked.

"I had had enough war," Sam said. "Irene's father owned an airline so I got a job with that airline as a pilot. Aw Hell, I have a story about that job that will tickle hell out of all of you."

"Well come on and tell us," Landers said.

"Like I said, I was a pilot for my father-in-law's airline mostly because I had married his daughter, but

I was a veteran pilot from WW II. On a flight from Salt Lake to Denver in a DC-3 we were approaching Denver. Crossing The Rockies was a bit bumpy and the stewardess came into the cockpit. Her uniform was clinging to her body after her attempts to wash the vomit from an airsick passenger from her uniform. The wet uniform gave a perfect visage of her breasts, nipples and all. She came into the cockpit and explained the dilemma to me. I told her to take her uniform off so that I could hang it out the cockpit window to dry in the wind. She handed me the wet uniform and I opened the side window. After shoving the uniform outside I shut the window on the collar to prevent the uniform from flying away."

"Was the stewardess naked?" Zemo asked.

"She had on a bra and panties," Haskell replied. "I guess the force of the wind was too much for the window and the uniform flew away into the sky. I have often wondered if any of the passengers might have seen it in flight and wondered what might have been going on in the cockpit."

"I'll bet you had fun looking at a half naked stewardess," Landers said.

"I did find the situation comical until I landed and went to the door to bid farewell to the passengers. My father-in-law stopped on his way out and asked me about the stewardess. I wasn't aware that he was aboard. I quickly told him that she had had an accident. He didn't pursue the matter any further. When the passengers had disembarked I went into the offices and found another uniform, took it back to the aircraft and gave it to the girl. The dry uniform was three sizes too large for her, but she would have worn a tent if need be."

The crew went to their bunks after laughing at Sam Haskell's reminiscences. The gather lasted another week. Payday came three days later and Zemo went to town, this time with Jim Landers. He found the used bookstore that his uncle had spoken of and bought several used paperbacks. With nothing else to do he found himself returning to the Silver Dollar Saloon.

There were only two men drinklng. Zemo walked up and leaned against the bar. The bartender approached with his bar rag in his right hand. He swiped it across the top of the bar in front of Zemo.

""I know it wasn't your fault the last time you were here, but try not to get into any ruckus with Big Joe if he comes in," the bartender said.

"I didn't mean to slam into him as hard as I did, but I had to defend myself somehow. That is one big man."

"Do you want some more tequila?"

"I suppose so, but not a bottle full, just a shot."

Zemo put his bag of books on the floor next to him and started sipping the tequila. After three shots he reached down, took one of the books from the bag and began reading. The story started out with a fight between two stallions in a mountain meadow. By the time he had finished the fifth shot he could make no sense out of the story so he returned the book to the bag.

The tequila began working on his brain making him dizzy and unsure of where he was supposed to be. He thought about his uncle's admonitions and then remembered he was supposed to meet Jim Landers for a ride back to the Y Diamond. After paying his bar bill, he picked up the sack of books and asked the bartender for the time.

The bartender looked at his wristwatch and said, "Five-twenty."

His memory suddenly came back and he realized that he was an hour late meeting Landers at the service station. Nevertheless, he began walking there just in case Landers had waited for him. He felt himself weave as he walked and began to think he might be better off to take the bus rather than have the foreman of the Y Diamond see him with a belly full of tequila. He turned and made his way to the bus depot where he discovered the next bus leaving for the highway past the ranch entrance wouldn't leave for three hours. For a moment Zemo pondered waiting for the bus at the Silver Dollar, then his uncle's words flashed back to his brain and instead he went in search of a restaurant for supper. He saw a neon sign in the next block that advertised "Zorro's Cafe. Mexican Food Our Specialty", so he headed in that direction, still weaving.

Inside the restaurant he walked to a table and put his bag of books on the floor. There were a few people at the tables and some Mexicans that looked like cowboys at the counter. The waitress, a stunning Mexican girl, came over with a menu.

"Would you like something to drink?" she asked Zemo.

Zemo looked up at the girl and was speechless. He opened his mouth twice but no words came out. Then he looked down at the table. "I would like coffee and a steak," he said.

"We have *carne asada* with our special *chile verde* sauce served with beans and rice," she said.

"What is *chile verde*?" Zemo asked looking up at the girl again.

"It is green *chile* sauce and very tasty," she said.

"All right, I'll give it a try," Zemo said. "By the way, what's your name?"

" Alicia," she said smiling so that dimples showed in her beautiful copper-colored cheeks.

"I'm Zemo," he said. "I think you are very beautiful."

"Thank you, Zemo. I'll get your coffee. How would you like your *carne asada*?"

"What the hell is a *carne asada*?"

"It is a steak grilled on coals."

"I reckon medium," he said.

Alicia disappeared into the kitchen. Zemo sat in a state of confusion. He had just met what he thought was a ravishing beauty of a girl named Alicia who would soon bring him a steak for his supper. Zemo wanted more than a steak. He was glad he had not come to town with Frank Spencer because he would never have met Alicia. Frank Spencer was probably at the Silver Dollar hooking up with Lucy unless Big Joe Goodman got to her first.

Alicia brought Zemo his supper. "There you are," she said. "Let me know how you like it."

Zemo looked at the steak smothered with green *chile salsa*. Alicia had dashed to another table of four to take their orders. Zemo took his knife and fork, cut a piece of the steak and put it in his mouth. He began chewing the morsel and found the flavor a delightful experience. He continued eating with an enjoyment he had never experienced before. On her way to the kitchen to place another order Alicia paused at Zemo's table to ask if everything was all right.

"I have never tasted a better steak," Zemo said.

"Thank you," Alicia said. "I am happy that you like it."

"When do you get off work?" Zemo asked.

Alicia looked at the clock on the wall next to the door leading to the kitchen. "In an hour," she said.

"I would like to walk you home," Zemo said and pulled his left ear lobe.

"I live with my parents on the other side of the river," she said. "It is about a mile."

"That's fine. My bus doesn't leave until nine."

"Would you like some dessert while you are waiting?"

"That is a good idea," he said. "I'll have a piece of pie with ice cream."

"We have apple, cherry and rhubarb."

"Make it rhubarb."

"I'll bring it as soon as I wait on the couple over by the window."

"There's no hurry," Zemo said, and leaned back in his chair enough so that he could more easily keep Alicia in his view. He watched her take the orders from the couple by the window and followed her as she walked toward the door to the kitchen and pushed it open. He heard a momentary clatter of dishes and pots and pans when the door swung wide before Alicia disappeared. He turned his head toward the couple and glimpsed them looking at each other across the table. He wondered if they were married or just feeling in love with each other. Zemo wrinkled his forehead as he thought about how beautiful Alicia was. He raised his right eyebrow as he recalled telling her that he thought she was beautiful. He had never said that to a girl before.

Alicia emerged from the kitchen with Zemo's rhubarb pie topped with a generous scoop of vanilla ice cream. "That looks great," Zemo said, as Alicia put the plate in front of him.

"I hope you like it. My mother and I bake all the pies for the restaurant."

Zemo knew he would like the pie no matter what. Alicia waited as Zemo took his fork and cut a small bite from the pie slice and ate it. "That has got to be the best rhubarb pie I have ever tasted," he said.

"I am glad you like it," Alicia said. "It is one that I made this morning before I came to work."

Zemo recalled the saying that "The way to a man's heart is through his stomach", then thought that Alicia had captured his heart before he knew that she could make his favorite pie. He devoured the rhubarb pie a la mode and sat watching his already beloved Alicia wait on her customers.

Alicia returned to Zemo's table in her street clothes in an hour. "I am finished and ready to go home," she said. "Did you have enough pie?"

Zemo clambered up from his chair. "Plenty of pie," he said, as he took her by the arm and led her out the restaurant's front entrance. He didn't say much for the first hundred yards. He had no idea what he should say or even wanted to say. He had never been with a beautiful girl walking on the side of the road leading to the house where she lived with her parents.

Zemo saw the bridge that spanned the river and the row of small adobe houses beyond. Each had an area behind that looked like a wire corral for livestock. One or two had corrals built *estacada* style with pairs of vertical mesquite posts holding horizontal mesquite logs stacked in parallel. They were in the same style as the corrals at the Y Diamond only smaller.

An old Chevy Impala came toward them, slowed, and Zemo saw two Mexican boys in the front seat looking at him and Alicia. "Who are those guys?" Zemo asked.

"Joey Castillo and Roberto Aguilar."

"Are they friends of yours?"

"Never," Alicia said. "I know who they are because this is a small community. Joey has asked me out many times, but I think he is a loser."

"Why?" Zemo asked.

He and Roberto think they are the protectors of all the Mexicans in Rinconada. They only want to sell their "*mota*". They are dealers of marihuana. I want nothing to do with either of them, Zemo. They are really bad news."

Zemo heard an automobile coming from behind them as he and Alicia walked toward the bridge. The car stopped just beyond them. The two Mexican fellows got out and swaggered back toward Zemo and Alicia. Zemo pulled on Alicia's arm and they stopped to face the two.

"Hey, *gringo*, leave our women alone. Leave her be, *cabrón*."

The two bullies strutted toward Zemo and Alicia. Zemo handed her his bag of books and nudged her gently out of the way. The two aggressors approached. With head down, as he had in the bar weeks before, Zemo charged one slamming into the bully's solar plexus, sending him sprawling to the ground with the wind knocked out of him. Zemo spun around as the other charged toward him with fists up. Zemo blocked the boy's thrusting punch, threw one-two punches to his head and watched the swashbuckler hit the ground unconscious.

He turned back to Alicia and took her arm again. "Now let's finish what we were going to do."

"I thought you were just walking me home," Alicia said.

"That's what I aim to do."

"You really knew how to take care of those obnoxious fellows," she said.

"I knew I was right," Zemo said. "I had to defend you because those idiots might have done something bad to you if I hadn't 'settled their hash', as my uncle Bayard would say."

Zemo felt wonderful to have been able to knock out the two swaggering Mexican boys, but he wanted to take Alicia into his arms and join in a kiss. He put his arm around her shoulders as they arrived at the front gate to her house, and pulled her toward him. Alicia put her hands on his chest and pushed him away. "Zemo, please don't take this in the wrong way," she said. "I like you a lot, but I really don't know you. A kiss might lead to something I don't want to do yet."

She lowered her eyes, then her head, Zemo reached out with his hand and touched her chin. "Alicia, I agree with you because I know how I feel right now. At least, I think I know how I feel."

"I feel the same way, and that might prove dangerous if I were to kiss you the way I want to," she said. "*Buenos noches*, cowboy."

"Goodnight, beautiful Alicia."

She turned and walked down the path to the front door of her house.

Zemo sat in the café where the bus stopped to pick up passengers. He sipped a cup of rank coffee as he thought about Alicia and the fight with the two Mexican boys. Off and on he rubbed the knuckles on both his hands, hoping that the pain would leave. At five minutes until nine the bus arrived. Zemo approached and stepped aboard for the ride to the ranch road. He bought a ticket from the driver and easily found a seat. As the bus arrived at the ranch road, Zemo wished he had met Jim Landers for a ride home, but he was also glad that he had met Alicia. He walked with an ambling gate all the way with his bag of books and didn't care how long it would take him to reach the bunkhouse three miles away. His thoughts focused on the beautiful girl with whom he had fallen in love.

Zemo wished his uncle would leave him alone the following morning. Zemo was not hung over, just tired from the long walk from the highway. Uncle Bayard wanted to make sure that he got his nephew rousted out for the day ahead. It was one of those ingrained things that when someone recommended a relative regardless of age and experience, he had to make damn sure that the relative got to work on time.

In spite of Uncle Bayard's efforts to get him out of bed, Zemo rolled over and grabbed a few more minutes of sleep. When he finally awoke all he thought about was Alicia. Suddenly he cared nothing about the ranch or even Uncle Bayard. All he wanted was the beautiful girl in his arms. He sat down to breakfast just as the rest were finishing. Nobody spoke to him so Zemo ate in silence. Riding looking for strays until mid-afternoon didn't help him forget about his yearnings. Bayard could see that his nephew had something on his mind, but decided to give him plenty of space. By evening Zemo felt somewhat better and asked his uncle if there might be someone going into town.

"I don't know of anyone," Bayard said. "What happened on payday? Did you meet some sweet young thing and fall in lust?"

Zemo looked at his uncle but didn't smile. "To tell you the truth I met Alicia from Zorro's Café."

"She's a pretty thing, that Alicia Quiroz. She's from one of the old families around here."

"Do you know her very well, Uncle Bayard?"

"Just from talking with her at Zorro's."

"How do you know she is from one of the old families around here?"

"The Quiroz family migrated with Juan de Oñate to Santa Fe. After the Pueblo Indians ran off the Spaniards, the Quiroz clan went to El Paso but didn't return to Santa Fe. They came here and tried to raise cows until the United States grabbed all this country from Mexico in 1848 after the war. After that all went well until the United States Government insisted that their claim to their cow ranch was invalid. That was the end of the Quiroz cattle business. They never have recovered what they had before the Mexican War."

"How do you know all this, Uncle Bayard?"

"Like you, I read a lot. I especially like the history of the Southwest."

"Then Alicia comes from a Spanish family?"

"Originally they were, but the ones who went to Santa Fe with Oñate were *criollos*, or born in the New World."

"She sure is beautiful," Zemo said.

"I can't argue that. If I was a youngster like you, I'd probably hanker to get to town, too."

Zemo couldn't find anyone on the ranch that was planning a trip into town. He was plenty tired of walking from the night before so he went to bed early without reading the rest of the story about the two stallions in the mountain meadow. But, he couldn't fall asleep. Thoughts about Alicia flooded his mind keeping him awake and filled with desire to hold her in his arms. He wondered when he would find a ride into town to see her, and if the Mexican boys would try for him again. He hoped they would not, but he continued to doubt, and pondered how many there would be at the next confrontation. He fell asleep rubbing his knuckles.

Zemo worked with his uncle for the next month gathering strays, doctoring screwworms and trying to find a remedy for pinkeye. Next payday Frank Spencer stepped up into his Model "A" and was about to start for town when Zemo ran out of the bunkhouse waving at him. "Frank, can you wait a minute until I get changed? I'd appreciate a ride to town."

"Sure thing, Zemo," Frank said. "This old feller needs warmin' up anyway."

Zemo quickly changed into his town clothes and trotted out to the car where Frank Spencer waited patiently. They went to town and Frank lured Zemo into the Silver Dollar for a shot of tequila. "Just one," Zemo said. "I need to stay sober tonight."

"I heard about you getting sweet on that Quiroz gal," Frank said as they walked to the entrance of the bar. "She's a young gal but you're young, too. Watch out for them Mexicans; you marry one of their gals and you marry the whole damn family."

"Hell's fire, Frank, I haven't even kissed her yet."

They stood at the bar and downed a shot of tequila, cashed their paychecks and Zemo watched Frank pay in advance for Lucy. Zemo could see that Frank really had good feelings toward Lucy even though she charged for her "love".

They retired to the table that Frank usually occupied as he drank his tequila waiting for Lucy. Frank ordered a bottle and then filled the shot glasses. "You know, Zemo, this goddam cowboyin' is a tough life in a bunch of ways," Frank said.

"I'm beginning to realize that, Frank. How long have you been a working cowboy?"

"Hell's fire, as long as I can remember. I'm thirty-four years old and look fifty. It's just a lot of more of the same every damn day. You get up at four in the mornin', go out and toss some hay into your horse's feed trough and measure out a coffee can of grain. Then you go back and grab yourself a cup of coffee and a chunk of stale bread. You go back to the corral and saddle that cold-back sumbitch and put on your chaps and spurs. Then you lead the bastard out into the corral and climb aboard, and that knot head will just as likely dump your ass off into a pile of wet horseshit as not. You climb back on and maybe get the sumbitch to realize who really is boss. You settle in, head out and ride all damn day checkin' cattle and fences or whatever. You get back in to the barn as the sun is startin' to leave the sky. You get a pile of food down to last through the night, and go to bed tuckered out. Then the first of the month comes along and you get a paycheck. You go to town, cash the sumbitch and sit down to get drunker than a skunk. Then you go back to the ranch to start another month of the same and they call you an alcoholic."

Zemo almost laughed at Frank's tale of woe, but thought better of it because he knew Frank meant every word. Frank's story got Zemo thinking about a career as a cowboy in closer detail.

The young cowboy left the Silver Dollar and made his way to the Zorro Café. Before entering he watched through the plate-glass window as Alicia waited on customers. He crossed his arms in front of his chest and looked at what he considered the most beautiful girl in the world. He stood outside for a half an hour. The supper crowd began to leave. Some glanced at Zemo, who leaned against the posts that held up the front porch. He wanted to wait until he had the chance for all her attention before he went to the front door and entered, strolling toward the table he had occupied before when he ate the rhubarb pie. He sat down.

"Well hello, Zemo," Alicia said, approaching the table. "It has been a month since you walked me home."

"I couldn't find a ride to town untlil today. It's payday."

"Are you here for supper?"

"I would like the same as before. Do you remember?"

"Of course I remember. In fact I have another fresh rhubarb pie."

"After I have supper may I walk you home again?"

"Yes, Zemo. I hope those idiot boys are somewhere else."

"I do, too. Why are they so against *gringos*?"

"I suppose it is because they have been made to feel inferior to whites by the whites and even by their own parents. We can talk about all that later. Otherwise you will stay hungry for a long time," Alicia said, and left for the kitchen to place Zemo's order.

Again he enjoyed the meal and waited for Alicia to finish her shift at the Zorro. As they walked toward the river Zemo took her hand in his. "I still don't understand those two who thought they could whip me," he said.

"Like I said they feel inferior toward whites."

"How would they feel toward me if they knew I was half Ojibwa?

"What is Ojibwa?" Alicia asked.

"They are an Indian tribe. My mother is a full-blood Ojibwa and my father is Irish. I get my black hair from both, but my blue eyes come from my father."

"I am supposed to be Spanish, at least my father says we are. Our ancestors were with Juan de Oñate who conquered Santa Fe. Lots of Mexicanos say they are Spanish but have Indian blood somewhere back there."

"Hell's fire, I don't care about any of that stuff," Zemo said. "All I know is that I am Zemo Doyle and you are Alicia Quiroz."

"That makes everything far less complicated," Alicia said.

"Sure does. Let's take that trail along the river and see if there any fish there," Zemo suggested.

"My father tells me there are fish in it, but the water is too muddy right now to see them."

"Let's walk along the river anyhow," Zemo said.

"I think I would like that," Alicia said.

Zemo squeezed Alicia's hand several times as they walked along the path by the river. They came to a grove of cottonwood trees that were beginning to sprout their new leaves. At a clearing that seemed to have been caused by a flood years back Zemo tugged on Alicia's hand, put his arm around her left shoulder and drew her toward him.

"I think you are totally beautiful, Alicia," Zemo said.

"Thank you, Zemo. I think you are quite a wonderful half Ojibwa man."

"I don't know what is happening inside of me. It might be the Irish or it might be the Ojibwa, but I know I love you, Alicia."

"You are so different, Zemo. I found myself hoping every day that you would walk into the Zorro Café again ever since that night when those idiot boys thought they could whip you."

Zemo stopped walking, pulled Alicia into his arms and kissed her. She encircled his waist with her arms and after the kiss put her head against his chest. "Wow," she whispered. "You took my breath away, Zemo."

"That was my breathtaking kiss," he said. "It took my breath away, too."

He led her to an old fallen cottonwood trunk where they sat with their arms around each other. After a half an hour Alicia broke away, but held Zemo's hands in hers. "We had better get home or my parents will worry. I told them about Roberto and Joey last time. I don't want to worry them. In my mother's young days when my father was courting her they had to have a *doña* to accompany them wherever they went."

"What is a *doña*?" Zemo asked.

It is most always an older woman like an aunt who chaperons a young couple. My mother told me all about that stuff. I'm glad times have changed in that respect."

"Hell's fire, how did your father ever get a chance to kiss your mother before they were married?"

I asked my mother that same question. She told me that most *doñas* are understanding and make sure there are opportunities for tenderness between those they are chaperoning."

When they arrived at the front gate to the walkway to Alicia's front door they held each other again and enjoyed a goodnight kiss. Zemo wished he could stay in Alicia's arms forever, and as he walked back to the bus stop he vowed that he would come to town sooner than next payday.

After buying his bus ticket Zemo noticed a poster on one wall announcing a rodeo to be held three weeks from Saturday at an arena on the south side of Rinconada. He made a mental note to ask his uncle how he should go about entering the bareback bronc riding and maybe bull riding.

Bayard scowled at his nephew when Zemo posed his question. It was during their ride out to look for strays from the Quarter Circle V.

"I reckon you didn't listen to a word I said on the subject of rodeo, did you, Zemo?"

Zemo looked straight ahead over his horse's head as they jogged toward the fence line between the ranches. He wished he hadn't asked his uncle and had sought out Frank Spencer instead.

"I suppose you have to go to the rodeo office, wherever that might be, tell 'em what events you want to enter and pay your entry fees," Bayard said.

"Do you reckon Jim will give me the time off to do all that?"

"All you have to do is ask him and find out," Bayard said. "I sure as hell can't speak for him. But, if I was Jim Landers I would tell you that you couldn't have any time off for such a nonsensical thing as a damn rodeo."

Zemo wanted to drop the conversation. He hoped they would come across a stray and direct their attentions toward that instead of more of his uncle's ideas about rodeo.

Returning to the headquarters corrals that afternoon they met Frank Spencer riding in from the opposite direction. They joined up and rode in together. After taking care of their horses Bayard ambled off to the bunkhouse leaving Zemo and Frank talking in the shadow of the barn.

"Have you ever been in a rodeo, Frank?" Zemo asked.

"A couple times. About that time I was beginning to train horses for a living and thought I could easily hold my seat on a rodeo bronc for ten seconds."

"What happened?" Zemo asked.

"The first time the horse never bucked. He just went into a spin and I was plumb out of the money even though I lasted more than ten seconds. The judges place you on how well you make the bronc buck as well as if you stay aboard the limit. The second time that outlaw sumbitch farted me off before he'd gone five yards out of the chute."

"How do you like rodeos, Frank?"

"I don't have anything to say about them because I never go to any. As you know I find better ways to spend my paycheck than entering bareback ridin' contests."

"There's going to be a Saturday rodeo at Sonny Bill's arena in three weeks. Do you know where that is?"

"Sonny Bill Jenk's place is south of the railroad corrals. Are you figurin' on goin'?"

"I want to enter the bareback riding. How do I do that?"

"To make sure you get in you'd better go out to Sonny Bill's a week ahead of time and put down your entry money. Do you have a bareback rig?"

"No," Zemo said. "I have never been in a rodeo."

"I still have my old rig. You can have the damned thing cause I'll never use it again. I don't know why I've kept it this long."

"Thanks, Frank. Are you going to town this week?"

"All right youngster, I'll take you out to Sonny Bill's and see that you get entered, even though I think you'll regret ever thinkin' about rodeo. Let's plan on Saturday afternoon. I'll stop by the Silver Dollar and see if I can get Lucy paid before anyone else gets to town."

Frank had once been a racehorse trainer for a man who spent millions on the best horses he could find. Frank had managed to train two champion running quarter horses for old man Gifford. After ten interesting years with Gifford, Frank quit the business when Gifford died and his widow sold every racehorse in the stable within a week of her husband's passing. Ellen Gifford hated horses. She also hated Frank Spencer because he was a horseman. Frank decided that he would rather work for ranchers training good working horses than deal with the wealthy people who owned the racing stock.

Frank wandered around the West for twenty years always finding work with horses because his reputation for training them to work cattle followed him around. He had been at the Y Diamond for two years when Zemo showed up.

The following Saturday afternoon Zemo paid his entry money to a man in the rodeo office and put the receipt in his pocket. "Better get here early Saturday morning for the drawing. I'd say no later than eight o'clock," the man said.

With that business taken care of, Frank drove back to the Silver Dollar, parked his car out back and the two walked around to the front entrance. Zemo followed Frank through the swinging doors into the bar. They both stood by the door waiting for their eyes to get accustomed to the light inside. When he could see again, Frank glanced around and spotted Lucy waiting for drinks at her station at the end of the bar.

"Go get us a table, Zemo. I'll have Lucy bring us a bottle and glasses."

Zemo sat down and watched Frank take out a bill from the right front pocket of his Levis and handed it to Lucy. He turned and came to the table and sat down with Zemo.

"Well, it looks like we'll be stayin' here a while," Frank said. "I'm surprised Goodman isn't here early to try and snag Lucy."

She brought a bottle of tequila, two glasses and several slices of lime in a dish. "There you are, Frank. Three bucks."

Zemo took three dollars out of his pocket and handed them to Lucy. "I'll get it. You were good enough to take me into town, Frank."

Frank was already pouring the shot glasses full of the amber liquid. He licked his wrist, shook some salt onto the wet spot and licked it again. Next he took a slice of lime between the thumb and index finger of his left hand. Grabbing the shot glass with his right hand, he turned to Zemo, who had followed Frank's ritual. "*Salud*, bronc rider," Frank said and lifted the shot glass to his lips and tossed the contents down.

"*Salud*," Zemo said, but took a third of the contents into his mouth instead of the entire shot. He didn't want to get drunk before visiting Alicia.

Frank refilled his glass and downed another shot and pursed his lips to the sour taste of the limejuice.

"How long have you worked on ranches, Frank?" Zemo asked.

"I started out with race horses and then when my boss passed away I went to ridin' green horses for ranches. I suppose I've been doin' that for nigh onto twenty years."

"That's about like my uncle only he doesn't break horses."

Frank filled his glass again. Zemo sipped the rest of his tequila down and put his glass on the table. "Frank, if you don't mind, I think I'll wander over to the Zorro Café and say hello to Alicia," Zemo said.

"Just be back here by ten so we can get back to the ranch at a decent hour. I'll wait for you."

"Thanks Frank and have a good time with Lucy."

"You can count on that cause she gets off early tonight."

Zemo left the Silver Dollar and walked quickly to the Zorro Café. Peering in the window he saw Alicia waiting on a couple at one of the tables. Zemo walked in smiling. Alicia came over from the table and told him to choose a seat. Zemo went to the far end of the dining room and sat at a small table where he thought he might be able to talk to her easily.

"You are here before payday, what happened?" she asked, after she had put in the order for the couple.

"I came into town to sign up for the rodeo at Sonny Bill's Arena that will be in three weeks," Zemo said.

"I did not know you were interested in rodeo."

"I really don't know if I am or not, but I'll find out in three weeks," Zemo said.

"Are you here for supper?"

"I sure am. Bring me the same and I want to walk you home again. That's all I have been thinking about."

"Not all if you came to town to become a rodeo hand."

"I'm just in the bareback bronc riding to see what it's all about. I hope you will come to see me ride."

"It depends on my work schedule," Alicia said.

"I'll let you know somehow once I know when it's my time to ride."

"Why are you doing this, Zemo?" Alicia asked.

Before he could answer, another table of four sat down and she had to go over to take their orders. When Zemo's order of *carne asada* was ready, Alicia brought it to him, and winked as she left for the other table.

He enjoyed the meal and hoped that Alicia could find time to tell him about what time he could walk her home. All the time he sat at the table in the Zorro Café, Zemo Doyle could think of nothing except how much he loved Alicia Quiroz. He hoped he would win the bareback bronc event at Sonny Bill's Arena so he could take Alicia with him on the road to riches from rodeo. What Frank Spencer had told him led him to believe that working for ranches was not the direction he really wanted to go. Uncle Bayard had found his niche in society. Zemo Doyle felt he had a long and different way to go. He began thinking about the upcoming rodeo at Sonny Bill's arena and how it might be to be sitting on a bareback bronc in the chute waiting for the gate to open.

* * *

Frank Spencer drove him to the arena in plenty of time for drawing horses. Zemo had no idea whether or not he had drawn a good bronc that would buck his way into the money, or a spinner like that which robbed Frank of his entry fee many years before. Frank had little to say for the first time since Zemo had known him, and he thought maybe the old horseman was thinking about his life around horses as opposed to a life with rodeo.

Zemo felt disappointed that Alicia could not attend the rodeo. But, he also had a feeling of relief that if he didn't stay aboard his bareback horse for ten seconds she would not be there to witness his defeat. He felt himself cringe at the thought of defeat and became determined to ride his bronc past the ten seconds and do as Frank had told him. "Spur that sumbitch every jump and make him buck his damndest."

Zemo had drawn a bareback bronc named Flying Witch and would be fourth out of the bucking chutes into the arena. Frank had mentioned that the stock contractor had probably wanted to name the horse Flying Bitch, but that wouldn't go over too well with the audience when the announcer gave the name of the horse over the loudspeaker.

Zemo watched closely as the first three broncs plunged out of the chutes, heads down and fire in their eyes determined to unseat their riders. He watched how the riders spurred and moved with the horses to stay aboard. The first two didn't last the ten seconds. The third rider went all the way but his bronc gave out early and almost broke into a trot.

Zemo climbed up over the chute, handed the bareback rig to a handler and watched as the man placed it on the horse's back and cinched it under its belly along with the strap around the horse's flank to make sure he would buck. He heard the loudspeaker as the announcer, Dusty Rivers, announced his name. "And now we have Zemo Doyle on Flyin' Witch."

He straddled Flying Witch and grabbed the handhold in the bareback rig. "Ready?" The handler asked.

"Turn him loose," Zemo said, and the gate swung open.

The first jump Flying Witch took was a high one and Zemo wondered if he would end up on the arena floor.

He gathered his wits together and remembered what Frank had said about spurring the bronc's shoulders at every jump. Flying Witch switched into a violent sunfish buck but Zemo had felt the change with his knees and stayed aboard still spurring with all the energy he could muster. All of a sudden the bronc reared and pawed the sky with his front hooves, coming down in a bone-shattering landing. Zemo pulled hard on the halter rope and managed to hold tight, keeping his mind on the task of spurring the shoulders of the bronc regardless of what happened.

The horn blew, signifying the completion of ten seconds. Zemo had a sudden feeling of exhilaration after lasting out the required time. One more buck and he swung his right leg over the Flying Witch's withers and jumped to the ground standing up. The people in the stands screamed their approval of his ride. He walked casually back to the chutes to await the return of Frank's bareback rig.

The remaining six bareback riders had mixed results. Four didn't last the time limit and the other two had drawn horses that seemed totally disinterested in attempting to dislodge their riders.

Zemo grinned wide when the announcer told the crowd, "Zemo Doyle was first in the bareback riding."

With Frank's bareback rig slung over his right shoulder he ambled over to the rodeo office trying not to look excited. After giving the middle-aged woman clerk his name, she counted out six hundred dollars and handed the stack of bills to him. "Congratulations," she said.

"Thank you, Ma'm," Zemo said, and left the office stuffing the bills into the front pockets of his Levis. Frank was waiting for him.

"Beautiful ride, Zemo," Frank said. "You rode that sucker like a pro."

"Thanks, Frank. I won six hundred bucks."

"You deserve every dollar for that ride. I thought sure as hell you would fly when that devil reared."

"I just kept on spurrin' like you told me to do."

"Let's get back to the Silver Dollar, there ain't a drop of tequila out here."

Back at the Silver Dollar Zemo bought the bottle of tequila. Frank gave Lucy a twenty-dollar bill and made his "reservation" for the evening. Zemo filled the shot glasses and they went through the lime and salt ritual before and after downing the fiery liquor.

"Have you ever thought about following the rodeo circuit, Zemo?"

"Sort of," Zemo said. "I talked to my uncle about it because I figured it was the only way I would ever get enough money for a cow ranch. Of course he gave me a long lecture about how bad rodeos are."

"All I can say is the way you rode that bareback bronc you looked like a pro for sure. Rodeo might not be for me for a bunch of reasons, but I'll bet you would do fine riding like that."

"Uncle Bayard will probably give me another lecture if I tell him I'm quitting the Y Diamond."

"Bayard makes his choice; you make yours," Frank said.

"Right now I need to go over to the Zorro and talk to Alicia. I'll bet she will be surprised when I tell her I won the bareback riding. What time will you be going back to the ranch?"

"Probably around nine."

Zemo left the Silver Dollar and walked down to the Zorro Café. He saw Alicia standing by a table of four just as he entered. He sat down at the small table in one corner where, again, there were no customers. He wanted to tell Alicia about the rodeo.

She looked his way and smiled once he was seated. Returning from the kitchen after placing the orders from the table of four, she stopped in front of Zemo. "How was the rodeo?" she asked.

"I won first place in the bareback riding," Zemo said and grinned. "I won half a year's wages in ten seconds."

"Congratulations," Alicia said. "Do you want to eat supper?'

"I sure do. Bring me my usual, please."

"I'll be right back after I put the order in," she said.

Alicia hurried to the kitchen and was back at Zemo's table in a few moments. "I had a talk with Frank Spencer, the horse trainer at the Y Diamond and he thinks I rode that bronc like a professional. I'm thinking about quitting the Y Diamond and following the rodeos around the country. It's the only way I'll ever make enough money to buy a cow ranch."

"Zemo, we need to talk about this. I have seen a lot of rodeo cowboys in here and they are mostly broke. Broke in two ways; they have very little money and many have casts on their arms or legs. I don't like rodeos."

"You weren't on top of that bronc this afternoon to feel how great it was to win first place and a bunch of money," Zemo said.

"Hmm," Alicia murmured. "It sounds to me like you have really caught the rodeo bug."

The bell on the take away counter rang. "Got to go," Alicia said, and went over to pick up the plates for the table of four. After serving the suppers Alicia went back into the kitchen and waited for Zemo's *carne asada*. She brought out the plate and a cup of coffee, and then returned to the kitchen without speaking to him. When the table of four had finished Alicia came out of the kitchen, asked them if they wanted anything else and left the bill on the table.

The table of four argued momentarily about who would pay the tab, but a large man with a walrus type mustache grabbed it and after withdrawing several dollars from his pocket, proceeded to the counter and counted out the money. Alicia faced him through the window above the counter. "Keep the change," the man said.

Alicia thanked the man and went back into the kitchen for a few minutes. Poking her head out the counter window she saw that Zemo had finished. The restaurant was empty except for Zemo. She walked out to present him with the bill. Zemo looked up at her as he took hold of her hand when she put the bill on the table.

"What's wrong, Alicia. You look like you've been crying."

"Don't worry about it, Zemo," she said.

"Well, I am worried about it. Why have you been crying? Can we talk about it when I walk you home?"

"I am sorry, Zemo, but I don't want you to walk me home tonight. I think we need to stop seeing each other."

"Why this, all of a sudden?"

"Because I love you, Zemo. I know I would not be happy following rodeos hoping you wouldn't break an arm or a leg. My brother, Pete, was a rodeo cowboy. He is now a night watchman at a cement plant because a saddle bronc reared over backwards and crushed his hip. I do not like rodeos. I do not care for the girls who follow the rodeos either. I do not want to become one of those women."

"I'm just doing it so we can buy us a cow ranch," Zemo said.

"Zemo, that is a pipe dream I cannot live with. I must say good-bye, but I must also say that I love you, Zemo Doyle. I bought your supper. Please don't wait for me to get off work tonight."

Alicia turned and hurried back into the kitchen. Zemo sat in his chair for a few minutes thinking about what had just happened to him. He took a five-dollar bill from the roll he took out of his pocket, left it on the table and walked out of the Zorro Café.

The following morning after breakfast Zemo told his uncle that he had decided to become a rodeo cowboy after winning the bareback riding event the day before.

"I don't know if Jim Landers will let you have enough time off to do much rodeoing," Bayard said.

"I wasn't thinking about staying at the Y Diamond."

"How do you expect to make a living?"

"Uncle Bayard, I made half a years wages in ten seconds yesterday."

"That might be the last wages you make in two years if you quit the ranch," Bayard said. "You'd best think this over a while."

"I have already thought it over. I figure to give Jim two weeks notice."

"You're a damn fool, Zemo," Bayard said, as he turned away from his nephew and walked to the barn.

When Zemo spoke to Jim Landers about quitting his job in two weeks to follow the rodeos, Jim scowled. "Zemo, that rodeo life is no easy way to go. So you won a bunch of money yesterday. You may not win again for a long spell."

That's what everyone but Frank tells me. Frank saw me ride."

"Well, I reckon you're going to do what you want to do. I'll be driving into town this morning if you want a ride. I appreciate you giving me two weeks notice, but I can see you're chompin' on the bit to start your new life. Meet me in an hour and I'll also have your check."

"Thanks, Jim," Zemo said.

He saw Frank saddling one of the green colts in the round corral. He walked over and stood nearby while Frank pulled the cinch tight.

"That ought to hold," Frank said, turning around. "Your uncle is sure pissed off at me. He wouldn't even say good morning. He saddled up and rode out."

"Jim Landers is driving me to town in an hour. I guess I won't be able to see Uncle Bayard before I leave. Thanks for everything, Frank. I'll miss you."

"Well, youngster, you keep ridin' those bareback broncs the way you did yesterday and you'll do all right."

"I'll do my best. You take care, Frank."

They shook hands.

"Good luck, Zemo."

Jim Landers stopped at the Silver Dollar and let Zemo off with his suitcase and bareback rig so he could cash his check. In spite of his lacking a week before payday, Landers had paid him for a full month.

"Thanks Jim," Zemo said through the passenger side window. "I appreciate it."

"I hope you do all right on the rodeo circuit. Where are you going first?"

"I was talking with a fellow at the arena and he said there's a three day rodeo in Yuma coming up in two weeks. I reckon I'll head over there."

"Good luck, Zemo. You're a good hand, so if you ever want a job again, let me know."

"Thanks," Zemo said, and touched the brim of his hat in salute, as Jim drove off.

Zemo stood in front of the saloon and glanced up the street to the Zorro Café. He felt sad and angry at the same time. He wanted Alicia to go with him to Yuma, but he knew from what she said and the way she said it that she would never come with him on the rodeo circuit.

In spite of the early hour the Silver Dollar was open for business. He walked into the bar and cashed the Y Diamond paycheck.

"Do you want something to drink?" The bartender asked.

"Not right now, thanks," Zemo said. "Maybe later this afternoon."

He put the cash into his pocket with the rest, walked out the door and headed for the bus station to buy a ticket to Yuma, Arizona. He tried not to look toward the Zorro Café. He wanted to put Alicia out of his mind. He thought of his uncle and felt sad that he had not had the chance to say good-bye to him. In spite of his exhilaration to be going to his second rodeo he had a somewhat empty feeling because of the way Alicia had broken off with him and the way Bayard had ridden off without a word except "You're a damn fool, Zemo."

The bus left fifteen minutes after Zemo had bought his ticket and arrived in Yuma close to nightfall. He found a small hotel near the bus depot and paid for a night. After putting his meager belongings in his room he decided to see what downtown Yuma had to offer in the way of bars that might attract rodeo cowboys waiting for the three-day show.

The Scorpion was the first he went into. There were a few customers but only one wearing a cowboy hat that looked like it had the right shape to it. The barstool next to the man stood vacant so Zemo sat down. The bartender walked over and leaned against the inside of the bar opposite him.

"What'll you have, cowboy?"

"Tequila," Zemo said.

"Any particular brand?"

"Just a shot with lime."

"I've got 'Viuda de Martinez' in the well.

"Fine," Zemo said.

The bartender brought a shot glass and then took the bottle from the well and brought it over to fill the glass. As he did that he also brought a small cup with a slice of lime. The saltshaker was in front of the man next to Zemo.

"Thirty-five," the bartender said.

Zemo put a dollar on the bar and the bartender took it to the cash register. As he returned with the change, Zemo shoved a quarter back to him.

"Thanks, cowboy," the bartender said.

Zemo went through the ritual, asking the man next to him to pass the salt.

"There you are," the man said, and watched Zemo perform the task to enjoy a straight shot of tequila.

Zemo grimaced after squeezing the lime into his mouth after downing the shot. He had decided to drink his tequila like Frank did and the rawness came as a surprise.

"That Viuda de Martinez is pretty rank stuff," the man in the cowboy hat next to him said.

"I'll say," Zemo said, and coughed a second time.

"I haven't had any of that before, and I think that might be my last shot of whatever you call it."

"Are you passin' through or workin' here?" the man asked.

"I came for the rodeo."

"What event?"

"Bareback," Zemo said.

"I came over for the bull-ridin'."

"Where do you pay entry fees?" Zemo asked.

"I'm goin' to pay mine at the Chamber of Commerce that's three blocks away toward the river. It sure as hell saves goin' all the way out to the fairgrounds."

"I reckon we have a spell to wait," Zemo said.

"Well, you know we always do if we pay our entry fees ahead of time. Otherwise there's no sense in getting to the place cause there won't be any slots left if you don't get that entry fee in at least a week in advance of the show here in Yuma."

"Where are you staying?" Zemo asked.

"I live in the back of my old pickup when I'm on the circuit. I hope the bulls are good this year cause that old pickup needs a short block and some new tires."

"How long have you been ridin' bulls?" Zemo asked.

"Since I quit college ten years ago. I won the bull ridin' in the college rodeo and bought the old pickup to follow the circuit. It was 'used but not abused', as the salesman told me. I work winters from time to time in a packin' plant in Phoenix cause I can't always count on the bull ridin' to make enough to put gas in the pickup."

"What do you do summers?"

"Generally I go north up into Wyoming and Montana. There's a bunch of rodeos up there and it's cool. This country down here is too damn hot for lizards much less for rodeo cowboys."

"I reckon I'd better get over to the Chamber of Commerce in the morning," Zemo said.

"That's a good idea and you'll be sure to get a bareback slot."

Zemo ordered another shot but asked for a different brand. He also bought a beer for the bull-rider. They chatted about rodeo and Zemo listened intently, never revealing that Yuma would be only his second rodeo as a contestant.

The following morning Zemo and his new friend Jesse Shaw, the bull rider, met for breakfast at a small restaurant before walking to the Chamber of Commerce office to pay their entry fees. For the remainder of the day they decided to look around Yuma, especially the old state prison, called The Yuma Hellhole by those who had been incarcerated there. They went into a cell that formerly held six inmates and decided that it would have been prudent to have been not caught committing a crime back in the days before the state prison had been moved to Florence from Yuma.

They spent two hours looking at all the relics and artifacts in the museum. The plank road that once traversed the sands of the Yuma Desert interested Zemo, especially when he examined the photographs of the dunes.

For lunch the two rodeo cowboys bought hamburgers and a six-pack of beer to take to the bank of the Colorado River and watch the flow of water heading for Mexico.

A week later, having seen all the sights in Yuma, they sat in the usual bar sipping tequila. "I'll tell you Jesse, this waiting around for the rodeo gets boring."

"That's part of it, I suppose," Jesse said. "Once in a while I find some day work when I need some cash, but right now I'm fine after winning second money at Sonny Bill's arena."

"What kind of day work do you get?" Zemo asked.

"Sometimes I drive trucks or even work at stockyards. They seem to have a little work they hold for people like you and me who are in town for the rodeo."

"I think I'll look around for some day work at the next town. You said that El Centro, California was next, didn't you?"

"Yep, El Centro's next, two weeks after Yuma. I found work in Holtville a couple years ago hauling carrots. Holtville's only ten miles from El Centro."

"How much can you make in a day?" Zemo asked.

"It's hard tellin'. Wages down here close to the border are pretty low, but I was down to water and day-old bread when I got on hauling carrots. I think I made five bucks a day. It got me through until the rodeo when I lucked out and won first day monies and that cured my finances."

"How long have you been on the rodeo circuit, Jesse?" Zemo asked.

"It's hard to keep track but as I told you, I quit college ten years ago and have been ridin' bulls ever since."

"How much longer do you think you'll be ridin' bulls?"

"Hell, I don't know," Jesse said. "When I started I thought I could ride the bastards forever. There's a bunch of sore joints hauntin' me that make me think I was dreamin' some back then."

"What would you do if you weren't rodeoin'?" Zemo asked.

"Hell's fire Zemo, what in the hell is a goddam bull rider gonna do when he quits bull ridin?"

"You have a point there, Jesse. I probably ought to think about what a bareback bronc rider might do once he gets fed up with rodeo.

"I started when we were all in the Cowboy Turtle Association. That started in 1936 in Boston Garden when all the cowboys put on a successful strike against the promoter because he wouldn't add the entry fees to the total purse. That jasper gave in and they all formed the Cowboy Turtle Association and had metal turtles that they attached to their belts."

"Why the name Turtle Association?"

"We chose that name because we were so slow to organize ourselves, but when we finally did we weren't afraid to stick our necks out to demand what we needed.

"Then, what is RCA?" Zemo asked.

"We changed the name to Rodeo Cowboys Association. There's dues and you get a card of membership. If you get hurt it's a kind of insurance. I always make sure I have enough money to pay those dues. You ought to join because a lot of rodeos are sanctioned by RCA and you have to be a member to enter."

"You have been riding bulls a long time, Jesse," Zemo said.

"Yep. And, I must tell you I am long overdue to quit. I'm getting' too old to take the chances of getting' stomped on."

"When do you figure to quit?"

"I was hoping that the one day show at Sonny Bill's arena would be my last, but I drew a lousy bull. Maybe I can make a purse here at Yuma."

"What will you do after you quit rodeo, Jesse?"

"Probably get a job driving truck," he said.

"Hauling carrots?" Zemo asked.

"That's a possible since we are close to Holtville."

The following day Zemo decided he needed to do something other than sip tequila and listen to Jesse Shaw talk about the old days of rodeo. He remembered how the art teacher back in Missouri had encouraged him to sketch with pencil and then India ink. The sketches and drawings of Will James and Ross Santee had inspired him and he enjoyed drawing horses, cattle and those who worked with them. He hadn't pursued his art since moving west.

He found an art supply store, bought a pad of paper, drawing pencils, some India ink and a penholder with four different points to sketch with. Zemo smiled as he made his way to the bus stop, thinking that with his joy of drawing things he would no longer find the waiting days boring.

The bus ride to the fairgrounds took twenty minutes. Zemo saw a lot of Yuma during the trip because the bus took a circuitous route that finally ended at the Yuma County Fairgrounds. A long banner hung high over the front entrance announcing the upcoming rodeo. Carrying his pad and pencils, Zemo found his way to the arena where he saw four cowboys on horseback practicing at the calf starting gate without calves. Zemo found a bench in the shade of a tall cottonwood tree outside the arena and started sketching the scene.

After he had gotten used to drawing again he began working on the individual riders on their horses. One picture was filled with the action of chasing a calf down the arena in spite of there being no calf to chase. Zemo had been around plenty of calves to be able to draw them from memory. Then the cowboys left the arena and rode their horses back to the stalls. Zemo continued sketching from memory and then practiced on drawing the calf chute. By two o'clock in the afternoon he recognized hunger panging away in his stomach. He put away the pad and pencils and walked to the bus stop. Before returning to the bar, he stopped at a restaurant and filled up on a large bowl of beef stew that came with a roll that the menu called "*pan bolillo*". The roll was slightly sweet and delicious.

Back at the bar he saw that Jesse had found another cowboy he knew and both seemed content to sip tequila and tell rodeo stories. Jesse introduced Zemo to the other bull rider. Zemo sat down at the table with them but just listened as he sipped his tequila slowly.

After one of his yarns Jesse turned to Zemo. "Where have you been hidin' today?"

"I went out to the fairgrounds," Zemo said.

"Anything goin' on out there?"

"There were some calf ropers practicing."

"That must have been exciting," Jesse said and snickered.

Zemo opened the pad and showed the two bull riders his sketches.

"Damn, these are good," Jesse said. "What in hell are you ridin' bareback broncs for when you can draw like this?"

"This is the first time in a couple years I have done any drawing," Zemo said.

"Hell's fire, I'll bet you could sell these easily," Jesse said. "Don't you agree, Dan?"

"They look good to me, but I don't know a damn thing about art," Dan said.

The bartender brought another bottle of tequila, put it on the table and took Dan's five-dollar bill.

"Hey, Smiley," Jesse said to the bartender, showing him Zemo's sketches. "What do you think of these drawings?"

Smiley looked at the artwork on each page. "These are excellent," Smiley said. "Did you draw these, Jesse?"

"Hell no, I can't even draw a decent bull anymore," Jesse said and laughed at his own joke. "These are Zemo's drawings."

"There's a man at the bar who will be interested in these," Smiley said. "Do you mind if I show them to him?"

"Go right ahead, Smiley," Zemo said.

Smiley took the sketchpad to the bar and showed it to a white-haired gentleman wearing a conservative silver belly Stetson with a medium brim. The hat was adorned with a beaded hatband. He looked intently at the drawings, turning the pages back and forth. Zemo saw him speak to Smiley and look over to the table.

Smiley came over and asked Zemo to come up to the bar to meet the man. "Zemo, this is Henry Montgomery. Henry, this is Zemo. What is your last name, Zemo?"

"Doyle," Zemo said. "Zemo Doyle. Pleased to meet you, Mister Montgomery."

"I like your drawings very much, Zemo. Where do you sell your work?"

"I just started drawing again, Mister Montgomery."

"I have an idea. I am president of a local bank and we have just added a conference room to the building. I think your drawings would look great on the walls of that room."

"Thanks," Zemo said.

"My bank helps sponsor the rodeo here in Yuma, and I think your rodeo drawing would be perfect. I just had this idea about drawings of all the events in the rodeo. Can you do that?"

"Sure," Zemo said. "How many pictures do you want?"

"Can you come over to the bank in the morning? I will show you the room. We can discuss how many and the price at that time."

"That will be fine with me. Tell me what time and where your bank is located."

"If you can get there at eleven I will have most business out of the way so we won't be interrupted. The bank is two blocks from here. Go out of the bar, turn right and then right again at the next block.

The River Bank is at the end of that block on the far corner."

"I'll see you tomorrow morning," Zemo said.

"Can I buy you a drink?" Montgomery asked.

"No thanks. I'll be leaving soon to draw another scene I remember from the last rodeo when I won the bareback riding."

"You should be drawing the rodeos, not riding bareback broncs in them." The banker said.

Zemo returned to the table and Henry Montgomery finished his drink, said good afternoon to Smiley, and left the Scorpion. Zemo went up to the bar and motioned to Smiley.

"Do you know if there's a store that sells pictures in town?" Zemo asked.

"There's two that I know of," Smiley said. "The Arte Place is on the far side of the Chamber of Commerce. I don't know the name of the other but it is out on the east end of the town."

"Thanks, Smiley."

Zemo returned to the table to tell Jesse that he would be back in an hour or so and then headed to the Arte Place with the pad of drawings and his pencils.

When he opened the front door to the Arte Place a bell jingled. There was nobody in the store that he could see. He stood by the door. Finally a thin man in shirtsleeves with silver cufflinks and a polka-dotted blue and white bow tie came out from the rear of the store and approached Zemo. "May I help you, Sir?" the man said.

Zemo noticed that the man looked him up and down as wondering what a cowboy was doing in an art store.

"I would appreciate some help," Zemo said. "I have a chance to sell some of my drawings, and I don't have any idea what to charge."

"Do you have them with you?" the man asked, putting his index finger up to his upper lip.

Zemo opened the pad and showed the man his drawings.

"These are quite good, Sir. You certainly have a talent."

"Can you give me an idea what they are worth?" Zemo asked, wondering if the thin man was going to charge for his advice.

"Are you planning on selling all of these drawings?" the man asked.

"The man wants a series of rodeo pictures, maybe a dozen," Zemo said.

"Who is this man?"

"Just a guy I met in a bar. He likes my work."

"Are you here for the rodeo?"

"Yes. I entered the bareback bronc riding."

"You're actually a cowboy?"

"Yessir, but I like to draw horses and cattle. My name is Zemo Doyle.

"I see," the man said, putting his index finger to his upper lip again. "I am Chauncey Oliphant. I think you should charge fifty dollars a piece, unframed, if your customer orders a dozen of this size.

"That sounds good to me," Zemo said. "Suppose he wants some larger drawings than what I have here?"

"Twice as big, twice the price."

"I sure want to thank you for your help, Sir. I had no idea what my work is worth because I have never sold any before."

"If your client wants your work framed, I can arrange for that," Oliphant said.

I'll let you know, Zemo said.

"I usually charge an appraisal fee, but you seem to be starting out. I would be interested in hanging some of your work here once you have delivered your series."

"That sounds great to me. I'll stop by once I have finished."

"I will look forward to seeing you again. When you finish the rodeo series, I would like to see what you can do drawing the Quechan Indians across the river."

"Do they have horses and cattle?"

"I am sure they do. They don't care much for artists coming in to their reservation and painting them, but you might gain entrance by wanting to draw their livestock. While there you can get a good look at them. They are an interesting people."

"That sounds like fun, Mister Oliphant."

"Thanks again," Zemo said, and shook Oliphant's hand. "I'll be back to see you soon."

"Zemo, you might consider that bareback bronc riding, as you call it, is hardly becoming an artist of your caliber."

"The man in the bar told me the same thing, but I get a lot of my ideas out in the arena."

"For heaven's sake, Zemo, you can go out to the rodeo without risking injury."

"I'll think about that, Mr. Oliphant."

"Good. And, good luck riding your unruly horse."

"Come on out and watch," Zemo said and smiled.

"I went to one when I first arrived in this miserable place. If you have seen one rodeo, you have seen them all."

As Zemo walked back to the Scorpion, he wondered why Chauncey Oliphant had come to Yuma, and then stayed if he thought it a miserable place. He was also glad he had not given Henry Montgomery's name to Oliphant. There was something in his tone of voice that told Zemo to withhold Montgomery's name or Oliphant might beat him to the bank in the morning to sell the paintings off his walls.

The following morning Zemo walked into The River Bank at exactly eleven o'clock. A nice looking girl at the reception desk asked if she could help him.

"I am here to see Mister Montgomery," Zemo said. "The name's Zemo Doyle. He is expecting me."

The girl rose from her chair and walked to an area that had several desks with people sitting behind them. At the far end of this space the girl knocked on an office door. She opened it, said something to the occupant of the office and returned to her desk. After sitting down again she looked up at Zemo. "Mister Montgomery will be with you in a moment. Please sit down and make yourself comfortable," she said pointing to a couch and three arm chairs in the reception area.

Zemo walked over and sat down, but he really wanted to start a conversation with the Mexican girl whose nameplate on her desk identified her as Noemi León. Zemo's thoughts raced to wondering if the girl had a boyfriend or might be married. He pondered asking her to have a drink with him, but Henry Montgomery's exit from the far office and his quick pace to the reception area interrupted Zemo's thoughts.

"Zemo," Henry said holding out his hand to Zemo. "It's nice to see you. Come with me and I'll show you the new conference room."

Zemo followed Henry to the opposite side of the bank where a carved double door with large brass handles seemed to beckon people to enter. Montgomery pulled a key ring loaded with keys from his trouser pocket, found the ornate brass one and slipped it into the slot. He turned the handle and the door opened. Henry stood aside and invited Zemo to enter the room.

Zemo walked into the conference room. He stood there for a few moments, saw that there were no windows but there were walls that would lovingly hold at least sixteen of his rodeo drawings. He turned back toward Montgomery.

"Mister Montgomery, I think I can make these walls come alive with my rodeo scenes."

"Zemo, I knew when I met you that you would be able to create exactly what we need in this conference room. How many pictures do you think would be appropriate?"

Zemo stood by the oval-shaped oak conference table and looked at the walls. After walking to the far end of the room and looking back he lifted his left eyebrow as he turned to take in another view of the room.

"How long and how wide is the room, Mister Montgomery?" Zemo asked, still sizing up the walls.

"I know it's twenty four feet long, but I need to pace off the width because I have forgotten the exact measurement."

Montgomery went to the end of the room and paced. He took four paces. "I would say that you could figure on twelve feet wide. The ceiling is ten feet high."

Zemo stood a few minutes longer moving his head from side to side. "Mister Montgomery, I think it will be best if I draw a variety of sizes depending on the event I am drawing. Once I have them finished I can bring them here. You can decide which ones you want and where they should be hung once they are framed."

"Will you furnish the frames?"

"Oh, no. I am not equipped to make frames, but you might talk to Mister Oliphant at Arte Place once I finish the drawings."

"All right, now we need to talk price," Montgomery said.

"Remember the sizes of those drawings you saw in the bar?"

"Yes, but they seem too small for these walls."

"I agree if you were to have only that size. However, mixed with larger drawings that smaller size might be good for variety."

"I think you're right about that. Where did you learn all this?"

"Just here and there," Zemo said, and decided he must be doing a good job so far.

"Fine, then what is your estimated price for all the drawings?"

"Here is what I can do," Zemo said. "The price of the drawings you saw in the bar is fifty dollars unframed. The next size larger will be seventy-five. The largest drawings will be one hundred. These prices are all for unframed drawings so you need to figure the framing costs as well."

"How many drawings are you planning?" Montgomery asked.

"I think I can do a very nice history of rodeo for this room with somewhere around twenty-four drawings of various sizes."

"What is the room going to cost me?"

"In the neighborhood of two thousand dollars, Mister Montgomery, depending on which sizes you choose."

"I don't exactly know what you mean," Montgomery said.

"When I bring the drawings over after they are all finished, there might be a few that you might not want. I don't want you to buy any of my drawings that you don't like."

"I'll tell you, Zemo, you are easy to do business with. How much deposit do you want for this commission?'

Zemo had given no thought to a deposit so Montgomery's question caused him to hesitate a moment. "A thousand dollars will be fine."

"That sounds reasonable to me. Let's go back to my office and I'll have a draft for a thousand made out for you."

"Thank you, Mister Montgomery. I would like to start an account in your bank since I will be here for a spell doing my drawings. I have three hundred dollars to add to your thousand in the new account."

"I think you are wise beyond your years. Your money will be safe in my bank and we pay interest."

"What is interest?" Zemo asked.

"Interest is a percentage paid to you for allowing us to use your money. We loan out your money at a higher rate of interest than we pay you. That is one of the ways banks make money."

"Suppose the feller to whom you loan my money doesn't pay it back?"

"That's the bank's problem, not yours. Your money is safe here and is insured by the government."

They concluded their business. Zemo had his first bank account and enough money to live on easily until he finished the rodeo drawings for Henry Montgomery. He went back to the art supply store to look at their paper prices and measurements and bought enough to get started. He also bought more pencils, an eraser and some pieces of sandpaper for sharpening. His mind focused on what had happened at The River Bank. He had already entered the bareback bronc event so he wouldn't waste that money, but his commission for the rodeo drawings made him swell with a different pride than he had had when he won the bareback event at Sonny Bill's arena.

Zemo bought various sizes of good quality paper, being careful not to buy too much because once he had finished the bank commission he might have to move on and paper would be an encumbrance while traveling. Then he thought about Oliphant. Should Montgomery contact Oliphant to frame the rodeo drawings, Oliphant might buy some of them and might even commission him to draw more subjects like the Quechan Indians across the river. He suddenly thought he might end up staying in Yuma longer than he had once anticipated.

Before going to the Scorpion he took his art supplies to his hotel room for safekeeping. While there he sharpened the pencils and began a sketch from memory of a big Brahma bull with spots on his face and a real mean look in his eye. After finishing the bull he took his pens of various thickness and went over the pencil lines. Then with the eraser he rubbed out the pencil marks. What was left was a pen and ink drawing. He thought about putting a rider on the bull's back but decided he wanted to draw Jesse actually riding at the rodeo.

Jesse sat at his usual table talking with another rodeo cowboy. After Zemo sat down Jesse introduced his fellow bull rider, Jonas Edwards, a short man whose hat looked like a giant flying saucer. Zemo told Jesse about the contract with Henry Montgomery.

"Hell's fire, Zemo, you'll make more money drawin' than you will ridin' those bareback horses," Jesse said.

"One thing for sure is I'll be one busy cowboy while the show's going," Zemo said. "I hope I can get most of the drawings started during this three day show."

"What about El Centro?" Jesse asked.

"I might have to go there for more subjects if I can't get enough here in Yuma," Zemo said. "I think

I'll go out to the fairgrounds tomorrow morning and see if there are any ropers practicing."

After breakfast Zemo caught the bus to the fairgrounds. He took some paper and his pencils, but left the ink and pens in his room. There were six ropers saddling up their horses when he walked into the arena from the bus stop. He noticed a few steers in the pen behind the release chute and wondered if this group of ropers would use the steers for practice. They were different men than the ropers he had seen before. Climbing the fence that surrounded the arena, he sat on top of the railroad tie post that held the top rail, which kept the woven wire tight from top to bottom. He watched the horsemen for a few minutes before beginning to draw. The riders stood their horses in a circle as they talked about roping.

Two young men in cowboy hats walked in from the horse barns and entered the pens where the roping steers stood switching their tails to ward off the flies that flew relentlessly around the animals. Zemo stopped drawing as he watched the two drive the steers into the long, narrow approach to the chute. Once they had the steers lined up and ready, one man called to the ropers. They broke off their conversation and two rode to the open pen next to the chute where the steer waited to be turned out. It looked to Zemo like the steer had done this many times before and knew what was in store. Zemo watched intently. The young man on top of the chute lifted the gate and the steer shot out. The barrier rope in front of the two riders snapped back out of the way and the ropers spurred their horses into the chase. Zemo watched carefully to capture the entire movement between the riders, horses and the steer running pell-mell toward the far end of the arena.

The steer didn't make ten yards before one of the cowboys snared its horns with a well-aimed loop at the end of his throw-rope. He quickly reined his horse to drag the steer so that the heeler could put his loop around the bovine's hind legs and between the two of them stretch the animal so that it fell to the floor of the arena. The cowboy who had roped the steer's head vaulted from his saddle with a short rope in his mouth. Arriving at the downed animal, he took the short rope from his mouth and wrapped it around the steer's hind legs tying a square knot and throwing his arms in the air to show he had finished.

Zemo thought about the pictures for the conference room and decided to watch the rest of the practice session before attempting any drawing. He had roped cattle out on the range but never in an arena and he could see there was a distinct difference. There were no bushes, trees or boulders in the arena; nothing to dodge or evade. Out on the range it was almost always necessary to ride slowly toward the target animal and try to encourage it to an area where the brush wasn't thick in order to get a throw at the head or heels, whichever was in the clear to rope. Roping the head was preferable, but if the bovine had its head in a bush with its hind legs free, go for the heels. That was better than allowing the animal to run off without getting done what needed to be done, such as doctoring for worms or pinkeye. Roping in an arena was a different game altogether. His thoughts flew back to the wild maverick bull he and his uncle had roped and dragged back to headquarters.

When it came to rodeo Zemo was a bareback bronc rider, not a team roper, so he needed to observe all the events in order to get the drawings done for his art client. He watched the practice session, which ended at noon. He took the bus back to town and without pausing for a meal, began drawing his images onto the paper. Before he was too tired to draw further roping scenes he had seven drawings telling the story of team roping. He decided to fill in more details after watching the performances during the rodeo.

During the first day of the rodeo Zemo kept busy drawing the various events. Completely involved with his observations of the events he almost missed his turn at bareback riding. He struggled to keep his mind on the bronc instead of his drawing, but his mount was a big speckled horse that charged out away from the chute and stopped so abruptly that Zemo flew over his head and landed on his back on the smelly ground of the rodeo arena. After catching his breath Zemo scrambled to his feet, and returned to the safety of the top rail of the fence. He sat there for a short while and tried to figure out his poor ride, concluding that he was more focused on the drawing project than on his event.

In spite of his disappointing ride, Zemo continued watching the other events closely, drawing when he could from his position on the arena fence. What he couldn't catch with his pencils, he brought back to the hotel in thoughts, where he spent the evenings drawing what was imbedded in his mind. He began drawing from the perspective of himself as the bronc rider and captured what he had looked at from atop the speckled horse with the fiery eyes that pitched him off so easily, beating him out of his entry fee.

Zemo stayed at the hotel for several days perfecting his rodeo drawings. Instead of settling on one drawing of each performance, he guided his pencils toward different scenes of each event to picture what really happened, not just a single drawing of each event, He ended up with an average of four drawings for every event.

All the rodeo cowboys had moved on before he had finished his artwork. Zemo caught the bus to El Centro, but he wanted only to watch the rodeo, not participate in it. There were still aspects of his drawings he wanted to refine. He also wanted to draw with pen and ink, something he found difficult while watching the events while perched on the top rail of the arena fence. Roaming the streets in El Centro, he discovered a small art supply store that also sold paintings and sketches. An instruction book on pen and ink drawing caught his eye. He flipped through the pages and ended up buying it after reading about pen sizes and differences in various inks. Then he bought the pens and ink he wanted to use and added them to his growing collection.

Back in his hotel room Zemo got to work practicing with his new pens and ink, sketching from his pencil drawings of various rodeo events. After three, he compared them with the pencil drawings and squinted as he looked at them. He decided to continue with the pen and ink drawings rather than find his friends in whatever bar they had chosen to spend their last afternoon before the rodeo opened the following morning. By evening he had completed six pen and inks of various events and felt good about his work. Having worked around livestock much of his life, accomplishing the right lines for the running action of animal legs came easy to Zemo. By the time the El Centro rodeo ended he had finished thirty-eight drawings. He had also changed the pencil drawings that he had started in Yuma by going over the pencil lines with ink. Once the ink had dried thoroughly he rubbed out the remaining pencil lines with his kneaded eraser.

After packaging the drawings and his belongings he took the bus back to Yuma, looking forward to delivering the drawings to Henry Montgomery, the banker. Arriving after the bank closed, Zemo checked into the same small hotel and put the drawings on top of the dresser where he hoped they would be safe. He felt the need for companionship so he made his way to the Scorpion Bar. Upon entering he noticed that it was not quite the same as when the rodeo was going on. Most of the patrons were either older cowmen or merchants of the town. He took a stool at the bar and asked Smiley for a shot of tequila.

"Hey, Zemo, how's it goin'?" Smiley asked.

"I got a bunch of drawings done in El Centro for Mr. Montgomery, but I didn't enter the bareback event cause I wanted to keep my mind on the sketches," Zemo said.

"He was in here a while back as usual, but he went on home," Smiley said. You'll probably be better off catching him at the bank in the morning."

"It seems strange in here without all those rodeo cowboys," Zemo said.

"This is the way it is all year long until rodeo time, then all hell can break loose."

"It didn't seem too wild this year."

"You should have been here last year when that big bull dogger, Luke Hensley, threw two bronc riders through the door and stomped them both unconscious out on the sidewalk."

"I didn't hear about that," Zemo said.

"The boys don't talk about it because Luke got himself killed in a car smashup two weeks after the rodeo. The two bronc riders were in the other car and didn't have so much as a scratch. It all happened out on the dunes."

"What happened to the bronc riders?"

"They didn't show up this year."

After breakfast the following morning Zemo walked along the Colorado River for an hour hoping that Henry Montgomery would be at the bank when it opened. He didn't know that being on time was Henry Montgomery's absolute insistence not only for his employees but also for himself. The doors opened promptly at 10:00 AM, and it was Henry who unlocked the brass lock in case anyone was waiting. He wanted to be the first to greet his customers.

Zemo was the only person waiting. "Good morning, Mr. Montgomery," he said.

"Well, well, Zemo, it's nice to see you. Do you have my sketches?"

"I sure do," he said, patting the package.

"Wonderful," the banker said. "Come in and let me have a look at them. I think it would be a good idea to look at them in the conference room where they will be hung."

Zemo followed Montgomery to the conference room door that the banker unlocked with the massive key. The conference table had been placed in the middle of the room, but the chairs had not yet arrived. Zemo put the package on the table and opened it carefully as if it held a treasure. Then he took the pen and inks out and laid them in a row along the outer edge of the long table. After placing the last of the pictures at the far end, Zemo looked up and saw Montgomery with his left hand encircling his chin. He stood there a few moments before walking around the table looking at Zemo's work without saying a word. When he had seen all of the work he stood with his left hand still around his chin and his right hand holding his left elbow.

"Is there something wrong?" Zemo asked.

Montgomery hesitated then looked up. "I am so sorry, Zemo, but I thought you were to draw the pictures in pencil, not ink."

"I did a bunch in pencil first and then inked in the lines. I think they look better in ink."

"I am sorry to say that I do not agree. I have always admired drawings done with pencil. Your forms are very good, even excellent, but I must have them in pencil. Are you willing to do that?"

"It looks like I have no other choice. It will take me some time to do these all over in pencil," Zemo said.

"Good, take all the time you need because I want them to look like the sketch I saw in The Scorpion Bar."

"What am I to do with these ink drawings?"

"That is entirely up to you because I cannot accept them."

Zemo gathered his pen and ink drawings, put them back into the package, and left the bank crestfallen. He had thought that he would have a nice payday. As he headed toward the hotel he suddenly decided to go Chauncey Oliphant's gallery to see what he could do about selling the pen and ink drawings.

Again the bell jingled when he opened the door and Chauncey came out of his office. "Well, hello, Zemo Doyle. I have been wondering if I would see you again."

"I went to El Centro and got all the drawings done, but Mr. Montgomery wants them all in pencil. I thought pen and ink would look better on his conference room walls than pencil sketches. I would have sold them at the same price."

"May I see them?" Chauncey asked.

"Sure," Zemo said as he started unwrapping the package again.

"My, my, these are excellent," Oliphant said. "I think they are much better than pencil sketches. I wonder what in the world Henry Montgomery is thinking."

"I don't know, but all I know is I have to do these all over in pencil before I can get paid," Zemo said.

"Hmm," Chauncey mused. "I think I would like to offer you a deal on these, Zemo. Do you have a place to work where you can do these all over in pencil?"

"Just my hotel room or The Scorpion Bar."

"All right, here is my proposition. I will set up a table here in the gallery where you can work. I will either buy these pen and inks or you can consign them. I will advertise that you are here working and would be glad to meet anyone interested in drawings of rodeo. In this manner I may be able to attract legitimate buyers instead of drapery pinchers."

"What do you mean by consign? And, what are drapery pinchers?"

"First of all, how much do you want for your work?" Oliphant asked.

"You told me the pencil sketches are worth fifty dollars so what are the pen and ink drawings worth, more?"

"I can probably sell them retail for forty for the larger ones down to thirty for the smaller pieces. As consignments you would get sixty percent and I would keep forty percent after a sale. If you want cash, I will give you fifty percent and the pictures belong to me to sell at whatever price I want to put on them."

"I would prefer cash, but I think twenty-five dollars apiece is fair."

"Will you agree to work here on those pencil renditions?"

"That will be fine," Zemo said.

"All right, let's count them and I will write you a check. This will be funny because the check is on Henry Montgomery's bank."

Zemo returned Oliphant's grin. "He is bound to notice me come in the bank to deposit the check," Zemo said. "I'll get my drawing stuff and be back as soon as I can."

"There's no hurry because I have to get some advertising copy made for the paper so people will come in to see you work. It will be in tomorrow's newspaper. By the way does it bother you to have people rubber-necking while you draw?"

"I don't exactly know what you're talking about."

"Standing in back of you as you draw, watching every line you make on the paper."

"Hell's fire, I don't rightly know because I have never drawn in a place like this."

"Some stick around a while, others are just curious as to the nature of artistry. Keep your mind on your drawing and pretend nobody is near," Oliphant said. "By the way, "drapery pinchers" are people that come in the gallery, look around and sigh, but never buy anything."

Zemo arrived at the bank while Montgomery was still behind his desk instead of on a barstool in the Scorpion Bar. He glanced over and Montgomery gave him a quick wave. Zemo went to the teller and deposited Oliphant's check in his account. When he turned to leave Montgomery blocked his way as he offered his hand.

"Well Zemo, how are you coming along with the pencil sketches?"

"I haven't had time to start them but as soon as I leave here and get my drawing stuff, I'll be working on them over at Arte Place."

"That sounds good," Montgomery said. "When you have a few done bring them around for me to see."

"Here or at The Scorpion?"

"Better to bring them here, Zemo."

"I should have some finished in a couple of days if there are not too many people rubber-necking."

"I'm here every day," Montgomery said, and returned to his desk.

Zemo wondered how long it would be after he left The River Bank before Montgomery went to the teller's cage to find out about his deposit. He threw back his shoulders and walked to the door, enjoying what he had just done. He hurried to the hotel, bundled up his drawing equipment, and returned to the gallery where Oliphant showed him to a small room off the main gallery where there was a table and chair. Zemo noticed that patrons could easily see him working through the glass window separating the room from the gallery.

Sitting at the table, Zemo looked up at the gallery owner. "Would you bring in those ink drawings? I need them to do the penciled ones."

"Oh yes, I'll go get them. But Zemo, I need to be able to sell them when people come in after reading the notice in the paper."

"I just need to capture the feeling again and then I'll be done with them. Most have good action stuff that I saw while sitting on the arena fence."

"How about as soon as you are finished with one or more of the pen and inks drawing give them back so I can sell them."

"Sure. As you said it will be tomorrow before the notice is in the newspaper."

Oliphant brought in the stack of pen and ink drawings that he had purchased from Zemo and put it on the table. "I'll leave you alone to work now," Oliphant said.

"Thanks," Zemo said, and began sifting through the sheets to choose which he would start reverting to pencil. He chose the ones he had done first in pencil and subsequently drawn the lines in ink, and began to touch his pencils.

As he tried to concentrate on his work his mind tossed him back to Alicia Quiroz. As he had lined up the paper on the table, he had wondered how she was and if she had found a boy friend. Squinting at the paper he was about to sketch upon he hoped she had not found a boy friend. He thought that being an artist instead of a rodeo bronc rider might appeal to her. Then he began the drawings after shrugging his shoulders to get Alicia out of his thoughts.

Oliphant stuck his head through the door once to see if Zemo wanted lunch. "No thanks, Mr. Oliphant, I have my thoughts together so I had better skip lunch and keep going."

"I'll lock up while I am gone so nobody will come in and bother you."

"Thanks," Zemo said. "That will help."

He drew the team roping series first, finding it easier the third time around. His speed had increased since he first began the project so he finished the first penciled piece just before Oliphant returned from his lunch hour. It was one of the longer sized pictures, fourteen inches high by twenty-eight inches wide. The next one he chose showed the two ropers with the stretched out steer in the arena with the header tying the piggin' string around the steer's hind legs. He heard Oliphant unlock the front door and walk to his office but he didn't look up from his work.

Several people walked into the gallery that afternoon. Oliphant met them after leaving his office when the bell jingled. Some paused to look at Zemo, but none seemed interested enough in his work to ask any questions. Oliphant beamed happily when one couple purchased a watercolor of the Yuma Dunes.

By closing time, Zemo had finished four of the pencil drawings. Oliphant came out of his office and over to Zemo's table in the gallery. "I have to lock up now, Zemo. You seem to have accomplished a lot."

"I think I did pretty well for the first day," Zemo said. "When do the rubber-neckers arrive?"

"I turned in the copy so my ad should be in the morning paper. At least they promised to try their best to get it in. By tomorrow afternoon we should see some visitors. Even Henry Montgomery might stop by. He has to be curious."

"I hope he doesn't mind me copying my pen and ink drawings to fill his order," Zemo said.

"He has no grounds to object to that after turning down the pen and ink ones. If he gets huffy I will just tell him that I bought them and have given you permission to do them over in pencil."

Zemo gathered his paper and pencils to take them back to his hotel room in case he wanted to work on some before he returned to the gallery in the morning.

"I'll see you when you open at nine tomorrow," he said.

"I might get here a bit early tomorrow so why not come in at eight-thirty?"

"Fine with me, Mr. Oliphant. I'll see you tomorrow at eight-thirty."

After putting his things in his room, Zemo left the hotel to have a tequila before supper. He sat several stools away from Henry Montgomery but the banker saw him enter The Scorpion and waved at him. Zemo waved back, but made no move to sit next to the banker. Zemo tossed his shot of tequila down as soon as Smiley put it in front of him on the bar. Leaving a dollar next to the empty shot glass, Zemo made his exit without having to talk with Henry Montgomery.

After supper he returned to his room and worked on his pencil drawings until he grew tired and went to bed. He had tried drawing without the pen and ink pictures to copy from and was pleased with the results of the three drawings.

Oliphant showed Zemo the ad he had bought in the local morning paper. He had never seen his name in a newspaper before and read the advertisement several times before settling down to his drawing. Secretly he hoped that nobody would show up until afternoon so he could continue making headway on the project. He figured that at the rate he had been going he would be finished in four days at the most. But when an elderly couple came in at nine o'clock after reading Oliphant's ad, they engaged Zemo in a half hour of conversation with Oliphant standing by ready to sell them something if they gave him an opening.

"I never rodeoed," the old man said. "I was too busy on the ranch doctorin' cows for screw worms and pinkeye."

"Would you like Zemo to draw a picture of you doctoring one of your cows?" Oliphant asked.

"No thanks," he said. "I don't want any reminders of all that work. I am retired now and glad to be living here in Yuma where you don't expect it to rain. I used to hope every day for rain. Now I am happy it doesn't."

Zemo continued his drawing. The elderly couple left without parting with any of their money. Oliphant stopped by Zemo's table. "Some of those old people spend money like water. Others are quite stingy."

"Sounded to me like that old boy had enough bad years in the cow business that he isn't overloaded with spare cash," Zemo said. He continued on a drawing of a mean looking Brahman bull with a cowboy who resembled Jesse Shaw doing his best to give the best ride possible without getting bucked off. By the end of the day Zemo had finished several pictures and had talked to several people who had seen Oliphant's ad and had dropped by to watch an artist at work. Oliphant sold three of the pen and ink pieces that Zemo had already copied in pencil.

Zemo took his pencils and paper back to his hotel room again and finished two more drawings before surrendering to sleep. The following day brought more visitors to Arte Place and Oliphant managed to make several sales of the pen and ink drawings. Having witnessed these sales, Zemo began to admire Oliphant's skill at selling.

By the middle of the afternoon on the fourth day of the project Zemo finished the last pencil drawing for Henry Montgomery. He told Oliphant that he wouldn't try to deliver them to Montgomery until the following morning because he knew the banker would be occupying his favorite stool in front of the long mahogany bar at The Scorpion.

"Why don't you keep drawing and I will buy whatever you do in pen and ink," Oliphant said.

"My pens and ink are in my hotel room," Zemo said.

"Then do some pencil sketches until closing and I will purchase them. It is because my ad runs until tomorrow. I didn't think you would finish so quickly. I would also like you to be here tomorrow if you would, Zemo. I have an idea in mind that I would like to propose to you."

"I'll stay today but tomorrow morning I need to deliver the pencil drawings to Mr. Montgomery and get paid. Then I can come back and do some pictures in pen and ink."

"Thank you, Zemo. I think you will like my proposal. It involves the Quechan Indians across the river."

When he was alone again, Zemo took out another piece of paper and began drawing Alicia as he remembered her. Oliphant returned to his office but the jingling bell summoned him before he sat down. Henry Montgomery strode across the floor heading toward Zemo.

"Why Henry, thank you for stopping by, " Oliphant said.

Zemo looked up from his work. "Hello, Mr. Montgomery," he said.

It was obvious that Montgomery had just left The Scorpion. "I thought I might come by and see how you're doing with my pictures," he said, slurring his words.

"I just finished them, Mr. Montgomery. I am planning to deliver them in the morning."

"That's good news, the conference room will look much friendlier with them hanging on the walls. Mind if I have a look?"

Zemo took the drawings from the box in which he kept them, and showed them to the banker one at a time. When he finished, he returned them to the box.

"Now that's what I wanted in the first place," Montgomery said.

Zemo felt himself give a sigh of relief. The banker turned to Oliphant. "Chauncey, these need to be framed for hanging, can you get that done for me?"

"Certainly, Henry, I'll be happy to do that," Oliphant said.

"Zemo, if you will stop by the bank tomorrow morning I will have a check for you," Montgomery said, turned around and left the gallery.

"I will wager that you are feeling quite relieved," Oliphant said.

"I'll say. I didn't know what he would say while I was showing him my pictures."

"This has worked out quite well for both of us. I bank with Henry, but he could have gone elsewhere.

He's basically a nice man but sometimes he spends too many hours at The Scorpion."

"He saved me from delivering the drawings in the morning. If I am still around when you finish the framing I'll give you a hand getting them over to the bank."

"Thank you, Zemo. I will appreciate that. In the morning I will talk to you about the Quechan Indians and what I have in mind."

Closing time arrived and Zemo gathered his pencils and paper to take them back to the hotel. Before supper he visited The Scorpion to have a couple tequilas to celebrate his relief. After supper he worked on his portrait of Alicia and wondered about her. He hoped that she would be happy about his change from bronc rider to artist. He drew a happy look on her face, held it away in front of him and smiled at it. He started another portrait of her with the teasing look she did so well. As he drew, he wondered what Oliphant had in mind about the Quechan Indians. He had no idea who these Quechan people were.

Before going to Arte Place in the morning Zemo waited for the bank to open by sitting in the small restaurant across the street with a cup of coffee. He had brought the drawings of Alicia to show Oliphant, but he had no intention of selling them.

After Zemo made his way to his desk, Henry Montgomery handed him a check for the balance he owed. "Thank you, Mr. Mongomery, I am happy that you like my work," Zemo said.

"You are a talented artist, Zemo. I hope you follow your artistic bent rather than try to win money bronc riding."

"I know a very beautiful girl who thinks the same way," Zemo said.

"Then listen to her," Montgomery said staring up at Zemo who had decided not to sit in one of the chairs. "Now go deposit that check in your account before you decide to enter another rodeo. I love rodeo, but I would never loan a dime to a rodeo hand. Pursue your art, Zemo. It might be tough at times, but you won't break any bones doing it."

"Thanks, Mr. Montgomery. I would like to just draw and even maybe paint pictures except I don't know how to do that yet."

"Find someone who can teach you and you will be painting before you know it. If you need money for lessons, let me know."

"Thank you again, Mr. Montgomery. I really appreciate your interest in me."

"If you enter one more stinking rodeo I retract my offer," the banker said, and glared at Zemo.

I'll see you down at The Scorpion this afternoon, and be pleased to buy you a drink," Zemo said. He went to the teller's cage to deposit Henry Montgomery's check.

Back at Arte Place, Oliphant asked Zemo to sit down in his office. "When we first talked I mentioned the Quechan Indians who live just across the river at the Fort Yuma Indian Reservation," Oliphant began. "I would like to commission you to go over there and draw portraits, shelters, basketry, pottery or anything else you see that would make a good picture."

"I have heard that a lot of Indians don't like to have their photographs taken because they believe the camera is capturing their spirits. Would that hold true for drawings?" Zemo asked.

"I am not sure. All you can do is go over there and ask. The worst they can do is say 'no'. You might start at their small museum and ask the woman who runs it. I went there once and her face would make a great portrait."

"How large do you want these drawings?" Zemo asked.

"I will leave all that up to you. First go there and find out if it is permissible for you to do their portraits. If you are allowed to do them, come back and we will talk money. The reason I would like this to happen is that I have a partner who runs our other gallery in Taos, New Mexico. I think Quechan Indian art would go over big up there whereas rodeo stuff draws clientele here in Yuma."

"When do you want me to go over there?"

"You could probably find out about permission today if you left right away. I suggest you take paper and pens and ink to show that you are an artist. In fact you might take that portrait of your girl friend to show them the quality of your work."

Zemo stopped by his hotel room to pick up some paper and his other things including pencils before walking to the bridge and looking for the museum that Oliphant had mentioned. Once on the California side of the river he found the tribal headquarters easily. He walked around the dirt streets until he found the small building housing the Quechan Tribal Museum.

Upon entering the museum he saw a rotund looking Indian woman sitting at her desk. She looked up when Zemo stepped forward.

"Good morning", she said. "Welcome to our museum."

"Thank you," Zemo said. He was somewhat surprised to hear the Quechan woman speak good English. "My name is Zemo Doyle and I am an artist."

He took the portrait of Alicia and handed it to the woman. She took it carefully in her hands and looked at Zemo's work. "This is quite good," she said. "Is the girl Mexican?"

"Yes, her name is Alicia Quiroz."

"Very pretty girl."

"I think so, too," Zemo said, taking the drawing as the woman handed it back. "I am wondering if I could draw the people here."

"I don't see why not, but some may not want their faces drawn. You just never know until you ask them."

"Would you mind if I draw your portrait?"

"Why would you want to draw me?"

"I think your face is quite interesting. I can see a lot of life in the grooves on your forehead and lines on your cheeks. There's more than just the beauty that is still there in spite of your age."

"You are a very good salesman, Zemo Doyle."

"Does that mean I may draw your portrait?"

"Yes, as long as I can finish my paperwork."

"Certainly," Zemo said and began arranging his paper and pencils on a small table from which he had a perfect view of the woman's profile. He began drawing in pencil and just before noon he had completed two. He wanted to give the woman one and he wanted to keep the other to show future prospects that she had given him her permission.

"If you will excuse me for a moment, I must eat my lunch in the back room," she said.

"That's fine. I need to go over these drawings in ink and that will take more than your lunch hour," Zemo said.

The woman left her reception desk and passed through an open door to the rear. Zemo took out his pens and ink and began going over the portraits carefully, yet swiftly. By the time the woman returned, he had come close to finishing the first pen and ink drawing. He continued for an hour and finished. Since she was still sitting at the desk he decided to start another picture with only pen and ink for Oliphant. That took him an hour to complete. He handed the woman her copy and thanked her for allowing him to draw her.

"Zemo Doyle, this is wonderful," she said. "Nobody ever wanted to draw me before. Thank you so much. I will show this to my children."

Zemo felt good about giving the woman his drawing of her. He returned to the gallery and told Oliphant about his adventure. When he handed Oliphant the pen and ink drawing, the gallery owner held it out to look at it and then placed it on a table in the main gallery to look at it from a different perspective.

"This is just what I visualized, Zemo. How could you capture that wonderful Indian look?"

"Maybe it's because I am half Ojibwa; I don't know."

"And this woman told you that you could probably draw others of the tribe?"

"That's what she said."

"Did you tell her that you are half Ojibwa?"

"No, I didn't need to tell her that. She liked my portrait of Alicia and knew Alicia is Mexican."

"Well, Zemo, what do you want for your portraits of Quechan Indians?"

"What do you expect to sell them for in New Mexico?" Zemo asked

"Unframed I think they should go for seventy-five to a hundred, depending on the size and detail," Oliphant said.

"We are talking cash as soon as I finish them, right? How many drawings do you want?"

"I would like to say as many as you draw, but I think we should start with fifty."

"All right, I'll take forty-five dollars for the smaller sized portraits and fifty for the larger ones. Pictures of baskets or pottery should be between twenty-five and thirty-five."

"That sounds reasonable to me, Zemo," Oliphant said.

"When do you want me to start?" Zemo asked.

"You have already started," Oliphant said, and grinned. "I will pay for each drawing as you deliver.

Zemo left the gallery. Early the following morning returned to the Quechan reservation with his pens, ink and paper. He had some pencils in case he met a situation that warranted it, but he wanted to capture these people with pen and ink. Inside himself he reveled in the fact that he might be able to portray their beauty, both male and female. He thought about their history that he had read in a brochure he had picked up at the museum. They had defended their territory against the Spaniards who sought to conquer their river crossing. They had not trusted those conquistadores nor their holy men. Zemo had read about the Quechan killing Spanish soldiers who, with the Padre Garces, tried to invade their land.

The Quechan people liked Zemo and gave freely of their time for him to draw their portraits. A few of the young men and women began following him around watching him work. He averaged four drawings each day. It would have been more except he spent extra time making each subject a drawing he or she could keep for himself or herself. But Zemo didn't mind the time he spent because he was thoroughly enjoying himself. Every afternoon when he finished drawing for the day he brought his work to Oliphant and collected his money. Each Friday morning he took the money to deposit in The River Bank. When he looked at his balance after the second week he thought about riding bareback broncs and wondered what his money supply would be like had he not shown that first drawing to Henry Montgomery.

After two weeks he had finished the first fifty drawings and asked Oliphant if he wanted him to continue.

"Zemo, I sent the first few to the Taos gallery and my partner telephoned this morning that he had already sold two without any publicity. I would say you can keep going with another fifty."

"After the next fifty I need to go to Rinconada for a visit."

Oliphant grinned. "I'll bet I know who you want to visit," he said.

"I figure to take her some drawings."

Zemo worked another two weeks during which time he made drawings of basketry, pottery and other articles pertinent to Quechan life besides portraits. Toward the end he felt some sadness that he would be leaving, but the thought of seeing Alicia brushed those feelings away. The day before he was due to catch the bus to Rinconada, Oliphant asked him to talk about the future.

"I am sure that between this gallery and the one in Taos you can keep busy should you want to return," Oliphant said. "I have sold six of your rodeo drawings and my partner in Taos has sold twenty-two of your Quechan portraits."

"I don't know if I'll be back soon, but I will be in touch. I enjoy doing business with you," Zemo said. "I suppose it all depends on whether Alicia has found a boyfriend who doesn't follow rodeos."

"I am certainly glad you changed your direction. You are far too talented an artist to risk your life in a rodeo arena. I wish you well and look forward to hearing from you."

"I was thinking about drawing range cowboys around Rinconada. What do you think of that?"

"I would say that might be a great series."

"Regular ranch cowboys have a different look about them. I have an uncle back there who has a lifetime in the saddle and the lines in his face that show the weather he has been through."

"I look forward to seeing what you come up with. Good luck and have fun."

"I hope to, but who knows? Thanks for your interest. Mr. Oliphant."

The bus arrived at the Rinconada terminal after dark. Zemo chose to get a room in The Hotel Congress as it was too late to see Alicia at Zorro Café. He left his belongings in the room, hiding the cashier's check he had gotten from The River Bank in Yuma between the sheets of his drawing paper. Leaving the hotel he went to see what might be happening at The Silver Dollar.

As he entered the bar he saw Frank Spencer sitting at his usual table most likely waiting for Lucy to finish her shift. It was almost as if he had never left and gone to Yuma and El Centro. Big Joe Goodman looked up as Zemo went over and sat down at Frank's table. Goodman said nothing, but gave Zemo an icy stare.

"Well, I'll be go to hell," Frank said. "How's the bronc rider?"

"I'm really fine, Frank," Zemo said as he shook hands with the Y Diamond cowboy. "How are you doing these days?"

"I can't complain."

Lucy arrived with a shot of tequila for Zemo. "Welcome home, cowboy," she said. "This one's on me."

"Thanks, Lucy, Zemo said. Turning back to Frank, Zemo inquired, "How's my Uncle Bayard?"

"That old rascal just keeps on going. He seemed upset when you left to go rodeoin', but he got over that after a while. Did you do any good in the arena?"

"To tell you the truth, Frank, I decided on something besides riding bareback broncs."

"That don't sound like the feller I saw leave the Y Diamond hot to make a fortune on the rodeo circuit."

"I've been making good money doing drawings of rodeo cowboys and Quechan Indians by Yuma."

"That's a long way from ridin' broncs," Frank said.

"Yeah, and I don't have to think about getting stomped or rolled on by some crazy rodeo horse."

"You're probably a lot better off," Frank said.

"Are you waiting for Lucy?" Zemo inquired.

"Not tonight, that damn Goodman got here before I did. I wish he'd go back to Connecticut."

"Do you still go over to the Zorro Café?"

"Yeah, once in a while," Frank said.

"Is Alicia still the waitress?"

"Damnit Zemo, I was hopin' you wouldn't ask me about Alicia."

"Why, Frank?"

"Alicia ran off with some feller from Sonora and got married. The folks over at Zorro's told me her husband has a big ranch down there in Mexico."

Zemo sat in silence rubbing his thumbs against his index fingers. After a couple of minutes he rose from the chair, pushed it back under the table and leaned on the back looking at Frank. "I guess I should have stayed riding bareback horses," he said. "Good to see you, Frank."

"Good to see you, too, Zemo."

Zemo clenched his fists once he was outside of the bar. "Why in Hell didn't I just stay working at the Y Diamond instead of going off to Yuma to a damned rodeo," he mumbled.

He kept clenching and unclenching his fists all the way to the hotel. Once in his room he sat on the bed and put his head in his hands. His sadness turned to anger as he pictured Alicia on some Mexican ranch with a husband. Questions raced through his mind. What should I do now? Where should I go? He sifted through his stack of drawing paper and found the two drawings he had done of Alicia. Holding them up to view them once again he thought he had done them well, but wished he had sold them to Oliphant. Holding the drawings together in front of him, he tore them in half first, then proceeded to rip them down into small bits of paper which he tossed into the toilet in the bathroom, flushing them down the drain with a vehement pull on the handle.

Zemo thought he felt better, but he found it impossible to sleep once he got into bed. He wavered back and forth between blaming himself for his loss and wondering if Alicia really meant what she said about loving him. He thought about the way he had been so stubborn; how he felt determined to be a bareback bronc rider just because he won a little money in the rodeo at Sonny Bill's Arena. Then the realization crossed his mind that he might have followed the rodeo circuit for a couple of years and never won another dollar. He was in the middle of thinking about drawing portraits of cowboys and cowmen when he fell asleep.

Awakening to the sounds of people walking down the hallway, he began thinking about his future as an artist. He decided that his loss of Alicia might be a benefit after all. He was still free to go wherever and whenever he wanted without the encumbrance of a wife. After dressing he looked at the cashiers check, even though he knew the amount to the penny. He remembered the bull rider, Jesse Shaw, driving his battered old pickup truck from rodeo to rodeo sleeping in the compartment he had built onto the bed to save hotel room expenses.

Zemo looked at the check again just to see again how much money he had made with his artwork. He had spent the rodeo money on hotels, meals and bus fare. He looked up at the ceiling of the hotel room. He didn't have any idea what a pickup truck would cost much less to have a compartment made in the back where he could sleep and even draw during bad weather. Things began to come into a different focus from the night before. In order to travel around to find and draw cowboys and cattlemen he needed more than a bus ticket. He was quite sure he had a market for his art with Chauncey Oliphant. So why not see if he had enough money to buy a pickup with some sort of bedroom on the back?

Zemo enjoyed breakfast at the hotel coffee shop, bought a newspaper, and went through the classified ads under 'automobiles' trying to find what he was looking for. There was one listing that he thought would deserve investigating. He telephoned the number given in the ad and learned that the pickup had sold the previous day.

Momentarily discouraged, Zemo looked at the ads from the various car dealers. Quickly he learned that the dealers were at different locations. The nearest was an easy walk so he paid his breakfast bill and started the adventure to see what the nearby dealer had that might suit his purposes.

He found the dealer's used car lot and walked around looking at pickups, checking the prices displayed on their windshields. Zemo had little knowledge of pickup truck values, or for that matter, any other motor vehicle. He knew how to drive and had a driver's license, but that was about the size of his knowledge of motor vehicles. He was looking over a green, 1949 Chevrolet when a man dressed nattily in blue trousers, white shoes and a white belt with a blue and white seersucker shirt approached him.

"Nice pickup," he said. "Are you looking for one? This one's a cream puff."

"Sort of," Zemo replied. "I would like one that has a kind of cabin in the back to sleep in."

"Most people take them off before they trade them in," the salesman said.

"Do you have any that still have a place to sleep in the bed of the pickup?" Zemo asked.

"Not right now, but you look like the kind of man who could build one easily."

"I probably could but I don't have any tools to do it. I'm an artist, not a carpenter."

Zemo remembered Jesse Shaw's old battered pickup with his housing in the bed and wondered how much it would cost to have someone build a similar structure."

"Why don't you get in the Chevy and try it out?" the salesman said.

"It is a nice looking pickup."

"It has a four speed transmission and a heavy duty rear end. That six cylinder Chevy engine will take you just about anywhere you want to go."

"I really want a place to sleep," Zemo insisted. "Eight hundred seems like a bit more than I want to pay if it doesn't have a place to sleep."

"Do you have to have a pickup?"

"That's what I have in mind. A friend of mine who follows the rodeo circuit lives in his and never has to buy hotel rooms."

"I have an idea," the salesman said. "I know a man who has a small trailer for sale. It isn't very big, but you can sure enough live in it. It has a kitchen and dining area and a bedroom with a bed. It also has a toilet and shower. Damndest piece of design I ever saw. He wants three hundred for it because he bought a bigger rig."

"Where can I see this trailer?" Zemo asked.

"Get in the Chevy and I'll take you out there to see the trailer. It's only a five-minute drive. In fact, you get behind the wheel of the truck and I'll give you directions. That way you can see if you like the way the pickup handles on the road. I sure as hell don't want to sell you a vehicle that doesn't suit you."

Zemo climbed in to the driver's seat of the Chevy pickup. The salesman took the keys from behind the sunshield and handed them to him. Zemo inserted the ignition key and turned it to the "on" position. Then he stepped on the clutch and put the transmission in neutral. Then with his right foot on the gas pedal and the starter knob, he pressed his foot down. The engine started immediately. Again he shoved in the clutch, shifted into first gear and let out the clutch slowly. The pickup began moving forward out of the car lot and Zemo steered it carefully to avoid hitting the other vehicles.

"Turn left when you reach Sixth Avenue," the salesman said. "You might as well stay on Sixth until we reach the river."

Zemo followed the directions and stayed on the road until he reached the river.

"Turn left and then when you see the bridge take a right. When you get across you have to go left on a dirt road that will lead you to my friend's place in about a quarter mile. How do you like the Chevy?"

"It handles quite well," Zemo said.

They arrived at the place where the trailer was parked next to a small barn and corrals. Zemo pulled up next to the trailer and turned off the engine. A man wearing a straw hat made in Mexico came out of the old adobe house. Zemo saw him and wondered how he could walk with the huge stomach that flopped over his belt so far that it looked like he had no belt on to hold up his Levis.

The salesman introduced Zemo to George Simpson who went over and opened the door to the trailer. "It's a dandy trailer but I need a bigger one," he said. My Myra can't stand to cook in this one cause it's too small. She's bigger than I am and that's saying something."

Zemo stepped into the trailer and looked around. Just as the salesman had said, it was a compact design and Zemo thought it would serve him well as living quarters. Outside again he looked at the tires and the taillights. "I would like to hook it to the Chevy and see how it pulls," he said to the salesman.

"That all right with you, George?" the salesman asked.

"Go right ahead," George said. "She follows my Ford perfectly and never sways."

Zemo went back to the Chevy, started it up and turned it around to back up to the trailer. As he looked out of the rear window he saw the salesman hold up his hand telling him to stop. The salesman approached the pickup and Zemo opened the window.

"The Chevy doesn't have a hitch," the salesman said. "I forgot to look before we started out here."

"What should we do?" Zemo asked.

"I suppose we could ask George to hook it up to his Ford so you could try it."

"If it's all the same to you, I would like to know how the Chevy pulls it," Zemo said.

"I guess we'll have to go back and find a pickup with a hitch," the salesman said.

"But, I like this Chevy," Zemo replied.

"I have one suggestion," the salesman said tilting his head and squinting his eyes. "Why don't you buy the Chevy, go get a hitch put on it and then come out here and hook this trailer up to see how it pulls. If you don't like it, I am sure there are other trailers for sale in Rinconada."

"That sounds reasonable," Zemo said. "Let's go back to the car lot."

Once back at the dealership Zemo and the salesman sat down in the small office. "The pickup is eight-hundred. Do you want to pay cash or finance it?"

"I saw a new one that had twelve hundred on it and this one is used and almost a year old," Zemo said. "I'll give you six-hundred cash for the 1949 Chevy, and not a penny more because it will cost me a lot to have a hitch installed."

"I'll bet a hitch won't cost you more than thirty bucks," the salesman said.

"That is an unknown until I go to some place where they sell hitches."

"I'll talk to the boss and see what he has to say," the salesman said, and rose from his chair to exit the office and seek the boss for a decision.

Zemo waited patiently, wondering what was taking the salesman so long to talk to his boss.

The salesman returned looking at the floor as he passed Zemo to sit down in his own chair behind the desk. "The boss says he already priced the Chevy low, but he'll take seven fifty."

Zemo got up from his chair and stood in front of the desk looking at the car salesman. "I said I would give you six-hundred dollars for the Chevy and not a penny more. There has to be another car dealership here in Rinconada. Thanks for your time."

Zemo turned to leave the office. Before he got out the door the salesman asked him to wait so he could talk to the boss again.

"You can tell your boss my original offer stands, and that is as high as I'll go."

The salesman returned more quickly than the first time. "You must be some kind of horse trader," he said to Zemo. The boss said it's a deal. Of course that doesn't include license plates and taxes. I'll write it all up. Will you pay by check?"

"I need to get to a bank before I can get the cash for you," Zemo said.

"No problem there. I'll get this written up and you can sign it, then get to a bank."

Zemo signed the sales agreement and went to the bank in the tall building in the center of town. He opened an account with his cashier's check from The River Bank and went back to the car dealer with his new checkbook. After paying for his Chevy he asked the salesman where he might find someone to install a trailer hitch. The salesman gave him directions to a blacksmith shop three blocks away.

The blacksmith, a large man with a gentle smile and soot almost a part of his skin, had Zemo's trailer hitch installed in an hour and a half. The cost was twenty-four dollars. Zemo remembered being told that the trailer took a two and one half inch diameter ball, so he added three more dollars to the final check.

Back at George Simpson's place Zemo backed up to the trailer while George stood behind giving him directions. Once the trailer got firmly attached to the Chevy and the safety chains hooked, Zemo asked

George if he wanted to join him for the test haul. Simpson demurred saying he had work to do. Zemo started out of the yard and down the dirt road to the first paved street that led away from Rinconada. Gathering speed, the Chevy proved strong and reliable on curves with the trailer on behind. Zemo smiled as he geared down to second on a hill. He drove out to the Y Diamond ranch road before turning around for the return to Simpson's to try and buy the trailer at a decent price.

As soon as Zemo drove into the drive, Simpson was out the front door waddling toward the pickup and trailer. Zemo got down and met him.

"Did your pickup have any trouble pulling the trailer?' Simpson asked.

"I had to go down into second gear on that hill out toward the Y Diamond where I used to work."

"You can expect that with only six cylinders," Simpson said. "I've got eight on that pickup of mine. I'll take three hundred for the trailer as is."

"I think that's a tad high, Mr. Simpson. That trailer is no spring chicken and the tires will need replacing before too long. Why don't I write you a check for two hundred and you sign over the title to me?"

"I have to disagree with you on the tires as there's plenty of tread on them. I don't intend to give it away for no two hundred dollars. I can always give it to my son who is about your age."

"All right, Mr. Simpson, to save us from standing out here for the rest of the day, what's your bottom dollar?"

"Make it two and a half and it's yours."

"Go get you title while I write out your check," Zemo said, and returned inside the pickup to write the check for the trailer. Finished and waiting for Simpson to get back with the title to the trailer, Zemo felt a rush of accomplishment. He had not only bought a pickup but a trailer to live in all in the same day. And he figured he had enough money in the bank to live for more than a year if he didn't sell another drawing. "Sure beats cowboying," he muttered just before Simpson came back with the title.

He was just in time to get the title transfer accomplished before the motor vehicle office closed for the day. The clerk wanted to know his address, so he told her to send it to him in care of Bayard Doyle at the Y Diamond Ranch. That chore over he checked out of Hotel Congress. It felt good that he would no longer spend money on places to sleep.

Thoughts of Alicia rushed to his mind. "Too bad she had to run off and marry that Mexican rancher," he said to the steering wheel on the pickup as he drove to a grocery store. It would have been fun roaming around with her in this rig."

He had little idea how much in the way of groceries he needed but once back in the trailer he was happy that the small icebox held all the perishables. The block of ice he bought at the store fit perfectly without having to chip any ice away. After stowing the groceries he drove half way out to the Y Diamond where he knew about a gravel pit would provide him with a place to spend his first night in his trailer. Arriving at dusk he cooked a steak and warmed a can of beans on the butane fueled stove. The small, round tank was secured onto the back of the hitch on the front of the trailer.

Early the following morning after a quick breakfast of bacon and eggs, he cleaned up the kitchen area before starting for the Y Diamond to see his uncle. Arriving at the ranch headquarters he was glad to see that all the hands were still at breakfast. He parked his rig and waited in the cab of the pickup. When he saw Bayard leave the cookhouse he left the pickup and walked to meet his uncle. "Uncle Bayard, how are you?"

"Just fine, Zemo. Frank told me you were back so I thought you might come by soon. What's this outfit you're driving?"

"Well, it's a long story. I quit the rodeo business quickly and started selling my drawings. I had a couple of really great commissions so here I am with what I bought to roam around in while I draw more pictures."

"You're full of surprises, Nephew," Bayard said. "I'm glad you quit rodeo. There are damn few who ever make it big it that game. The few who are good make it impossible for those who are not so good to make a living in the arena."

"I did a good job riding that bareback bronc at Sonny Bill's."

"That you did. I won't argue that for a minute, but quiting a good ranch job still sounds a bit stupid to me."

"If I told you how much I made drawing rodeo hands doing what they do and Quechan Indian portraits, you might change your mind."

"What are you going to do now with that rig?" Bayard asked.

"I will travel around to various parts of the country drawing horses, cattle, cowboys, Indians and even a few barns and corrals. By the way, I would like to draw your portrait, Uncle Bayard. You have a really interesting face."

"I've got work to do," Bayard said. "I can't be sitting around while you draw my picture."

"It won't take long, maybe an hour and then I can fill in what I didn't draw from my recollections."

"I've got to get saddled up and chase some strays back to that fool Goodman's place and mend the fence. How about when I get back to the barn this afternoon?"

"That'll be fine. There's a lot of stuff around headquarters to draw today," Zemo said.

Bayard trudged to the barn and corrals. Zemo went inside the trailer and sorted through his pencils, pens, ink and paper and reached for the 16X24 inch piece of plywood he used for an easel. He remembered the inside of the tack room where all the saddles were sitting on wooden "horses" attached to the walls ready for use. These "horses" were made from two-by-six lumber assembled in such a fashion to provide an angle on the top where the saddle would stay when placed there. On the front below the saddle rack there was a round piece of wood for a bridle or hackamore so the headstall wouldn't lose its shape.

As he left the trailer, Zemo saw Bayard riding out toward the Goodman border trailing a packhorse loaded with wire and a couple of posts. Zemo knew what Bayard would be doing because he had helped him when he had been on the Y Diamond payroll.

There was no chair in the tack room so Zemo carried a sawhorse in to sit on while he composed his drawing. He enjoyed sketching out the various saddle styles and drawing the bridles and hackamores. Behind the saddles on the wall were more bridles and hackamores that were not currently being used. He added those to the drawing. It took him two hours to complete the drawing.

Next he went out to where the baled hay stood stacked in the main part of the barn. There were two pitchforks, a manure shovel and some bale hooks hanging on nails driven into the inside walls. Some baling wire had been tossed onto a pile in the front corner. Zemo noticed that even though the pile had grown higher since he had been there, nobody had moved it. Bayard had told him that they kept the wire inside to keep it from rusting. There was always a need for baling wire on the Y Diamond.

Zemo started another drawing and included the baling wire and the tools. The drawing showed the wire next to the tools when in actuality the pile of wire was in the front corner next to the wide front door. He also drew a corner behind the stack of hay.

After putting the finishing touches on his drawing he returned to his trailer, made a thick roast beef sandwich and opened a bottle of beer that was cold from leaning against the block of ice that had somewhat melted down. Frank Spencer knocked on the trailer door while Zemo ate his lunch. He put the sandwich down and opened the door.

"Hello, Frank," Zemo said. "Come on in and sit a spell."

"I need to get over to the cookhouse and eat. I was wondering who was in this trailer," Frank said.

"I came out to draw," Zemo said.

"Nice rig. I thought I saw you this morning talking to Bayard, but I was too far away to be sure."

"When you're finished eating how about coming back so I can draw your portrait?" Zemo asked.

"What the hell do you want with a picture of me, Zemo?"

"I'm doing a collection of cowboys and ranch stuff, and you are damn sure a cowboy."

"How long will it take?"

"It shouldn't be a long time, probably less than an hour. I can fill in any details from memory later."

"That'll be all right," Frank said. "I just need to get to the Silver Dollar before Goodman gets there. In case you have forgotten, today is payday."

"I can't figure out how you can afford Lucy on cowboy wages," Zemo said.

"That's between me and Lucy, Zemo.

"All right, Frank, I won't ask you again."

"Thanks, Zemo, I better get going before all the steak is gone. See you in a little bit."

While Zemo finished his sandwich and beer he had an idea about the collection. Written paragraphs, short biographies or stories about the various people he would draw might add to the interest of the collection to buyers. He also thought about writing about the various drawings like the tack room he had almost completed. He tugged on the bottle of beer, put it on the table that could be lowered to the frame below to serve as a second bed, and thought about Oliphant. "I'll bet old Chauncey would think that's a good idea," he said to himself.

Frank returned and seemed impatient to get to town. "Why don't you go ahead into town, Frank," Zemo said. "I'll be around for several days. Come by when you get the chance."

"Thanks, Zemo. I am kind of in a hurry. I'll see you tomorrow."

After Frank left, Zemo pencil-sketched his face and old sweated up cowboy hat as he had observed minutes before and remembered from all the time he had spent with Frank when he worked for the Y Diamond. He left the drawing on the table in the trailer, and with his paper, ink and pens, went to the corrals to draw the loading chute and other aspects such as the squeeze where mature animals were restrained for all sorts of reasons, but usually doctoring or branding.

He carried the sawhorse from the barn out to a vantage point where he could get a nice angle on the loading chute and began his drawing. He silently wished that there had been a loading operation in process but he also figured that he could always draw that into the picture later. Once finished with the outside view of the chute, he opened the gate to the corral and walked inside to a point where he had a view of the chute looking down onto it. After drawing the structure, he began adding a line of cattle being pushed up the chute into a cattle truck. The Y Diamond cattle were mostly dehorned, but Zemo drew them with horns. He liked the result when he had finished.

He wondered what the picture might look like in color as he returned to the pickup to get ready for when Bayard returned from chasing strays and fixing fence.

Back in the trailer Zemo filddled with some details in the drawings of the corrals and began inking in the portrait of Frank. As he was finishing Frank's portrait Bayard stopped at the open door to the trailer. "Well, I got those rat-tailed, bone bags back in their own pasture," he said. "I swear that Goodman has no idea about carrying capacity. That country is eaten down to the nubbins and tromped as well. Damn fool!"

"How many strays did you have to work, Uncle Bayard?"

"It's getting' worse every time. I found eleven head in that country but I might have missed some. I'll have to check the new well tomorrow to see if any more came in to water. I need to have a talk with Jim about this crap. Maybe he needs to have Sam Haskell have a talk with that idiot Goodman."

"Do you have time to sit a spell so I can draw your picture?" Zemo asked.

"How long will it take?"

"Maybe an hour or so," Zemo replied. "I'll try to work fast."

"Well, where do you want to do all this stuff?"

"How about up by the corrals. The light is still good and I will have some good background for the portrait."

"All right, let's get to it. I need to see Jim Landers as soon as possible."

ZEMO

They walked up to the corrals together and Zemo positioned Bayard in front of the loading chute. The afternoon sun made some interesting shadows across the old cowboy's face and Zemo went to work to capture the mood as quickly as possible before the sun sank further toward the horizon.

The bust portrait finished, Zemo began another drawing of his uncle to show the chaps and spurs that Bayard had not removed before going to the trailer. The entire process took a little over an hour before Zemo felt satisfied with his work.

"All right, Uncle Bayard," Zemo said, as he gathered up his pens, ink and paper. "How do you like the pictures?" Zemo asked as he held them up for Bayard to inspect.

"You sure put a lot of lines in my face, Nephew," Bayard said.

"Go look in a mirror. Those lines are pure art because you came by them honestly."

" I have to admit, Zemo, you're a good man with a pen," Bayard said. "When did you start drawing instead of rodeoing?"

"I've been drawing for a while. I had a teacher in school that told me I should always draw. Well, I didn't always remember what she said until I decided that riding bareback broncs was not as easy as I thought it was after that first win."

"Whatever changed your mind, I am happy. That rodeo life isn't what it looks like from the outside. How long are you figuring to stick around the Y Diamond?"

"I don't really know. I'd like to draw Jim Landers and there's that old windmill and the corrals out in the Davis section that would make a good drawing. I may go out there for a couple of days after I draw Jim if he'll agree to it. I need to go into town tomorrow for supplies. My chunk of ice is about melted and I need some more food."

"Why not come over and eat with the rest of us?" Bayard asked.

"I know I'd be welcome, but since I am not on the payroll anymore I feel better making my own way."

"You always were an independent cuss," Bayard said, and grinned. "You sure are different from my brother."

Zemo went to the foreman's house and saw Landers' pickup parked in its usual place by the back door. He was glad the foreman was at home and he made an appointment to draw his portrait the following afternoon before suppertime.

After unhooking the trailer for the morning trip to town he drove away from the Y Diamond and past Zorro Café. He wondered how Alicia liked living on the big *rancho* in Mexico. He pondered stopping in for lunch, but decided against it because he didn't want to feel sad again. He enjoyed drawing and that had taken the place of a lot of past things in his life.

With a new block of ice wrapped up in newspaper for his ice box and enough beans, beefsteak and a dozen eggs that would do him for several days, Zemo drove back to the Y Diamond to wait for Jim Landers to return from his day's work checking pumps and water tanks. He had to make sure all the cattle had plenty of water.

Zemo spent the waiting time touching up the portraits he had made of Frank and Bayard. He left Bayard's face the way he had originally drawn it, but he put a few more flourishes on his well-worn Stetson.

Landers parked his pickup outside the trailer and stepped to the door and knocked. "You there, Zemo?"

"I'll be right with you, Jim. I need to gather up my stuff so we can go up to the barn."

Zemo had decided that he wanted to have Jim Landers astride a horse for the picture. He carried all the things he needed for the drawing session and the two walked up the slight hill to the barn and corral area. "Could you possibly saddle a horse and sit in the saddle?" Zemo asked.

"Are you going to draw me or the horse?" Landers said, and grinned.

"I'm thinking I would like to show you in the saddle but draw just part of the horse. The angle would be what I am aiming for in the portrait of a foreman."

"I didn't know artists were so damned fussy," Landers said and grinned again before going to the tack room and getting out his saddle. He walked into the corral and bridled the roan gelding he rode most of the time and quickly saddled him.

"I think if you stand just outside the big double doors, I can use the frame to kind of enclose the portrait. You will be above the doors because of the angle but Roany will be framed in the doorway."

Landers reined the roan so that he was in front of the big double doors that were open to the inside of the barn. "That's perfect," Zemo said. "I'll take this sawhorse around to sit on while I draw."

Zemo positioned the sawhorse and tried it out for the angle he looked for. "That's perfect, Jim," Zemo said. "Now if you look out toward your house it will be just right to show a foreman looking over the ranch he manages."

Zemo began. He wanted to catch the look that he felt so appropriate for Jim Landers before his subject tired and changed positions or the horse moved and Jim had to rein him back in front of the barn door.

The roan gelding stayed still and Jim Landers never moved until Zemo told him he could relax. Jim turned toward Zemo and smiled. "I never knew you were an artist while you were a cowboy here at the Y Diamond," Jim said.

"I wasn't," Zemo said as he turned the portrait so that Landers could see it.

"That's pretty damn good, Zemo," Jim said. "How long do you figure to be here drawing at the Y Diamond?"

"I have no idea," Zemo replied. "There are lots of things I know about here that I want to draw. I thought I would like to go out to the old dry well at the Moore section and draw that old windmill and those old mesquite corrals there."

"When are you going out there?"

"I think I'll finish up around headquarters in a couple of days and then go out there for a spell."

"I'll tell you, Zemo, I would sure like to have you back on the payroll as a cowboy. I'll raise your wages to a hundred twenty-five a month."

"I appreciate that, Jim, but I feel a real need to keep drawing. When I left here with that purse money from Sonny Bill's rodeo and a month's wages, I went to Yuma thinking I was going to cut a fat hog in the ass rodeoing. After one bum ride I realized that I could ride bareback broncs for a year and never win back my entry fees. I quit and went to drawing. I got lucky and got a commission right off and now I have a bank account and the pickup and trailer to travel with and live in. And, I don't need to worry about broken bones or scattered brains."

"Just thought I'd ask. I can't say I disagree with you. You damn sure can draw. My daughter Maggie will be here three days from now. She's on break from art school in California. I'll send her out to the Moore windmill and you two can talk about art. She's good at watercolors."

"I'd like that, Jim," Zemo said. "It's difficult to find anyone to talk with about art. Actually, I have no idea what I would talk with your daughter about because I never had any schooling in art."

"All the more reason you should get to know Maggie. She can talk art until I fall asleep on the couch."

"I'll try to make another drawing of you tonight and drop it off at your house in the morning," Zemo said. Underneath, he wondered what Maggie Landers was like and looked forward to meeting her. His thoughts flashed back to Alicia and he felt a pang of sadness he had not felt in several days.

Inside the trailer Zemo made another portrait of Jim Landers without the horse. In some ways he liked it better than the drawing he had done by the barn, so he drew another to give to the foreman. The following morning Zemo arranged things in the trailer for the drive to Moore Well. On the way he stopped at the foreman's house and gave him the portrait.

"Thanks, Zemo. This is really nice. I'll show it to Maggie when she gets here from California."

"Glad you like it, Jim," Zemo said. I'm heading out to the Moore Well to do some drawing. I'll probably stay there a few days."

"Let me know if you see anything that needs tending to."

"Sure thing," Zemo said and returned to his pickup.

Arriving at the well and corrals that had once been the center of Henry Moore's homestead, Zemo parked his rig on the level ground that formed a small flat area fifty yards from the corrals. After stepping out of the pickup he looked at the ground and saw that he had parked on what had once been Henry Moore's house. The foundation had sunk and was almost hidden from view, but Zemo saw where it had once formed the base of the dwelling. Leaving the pickup and trailer he wandered down to check out the corrals and the old windmill.

Right off he saw that several blades from the fan had come loose and dropped down but were still attached somehow. He wondered why they hadn't blown away long ago. The brand name, "Aeromotor" was badly faded on the broken, sagging tail, but was still visible. The sucker rod had been disconnected and the galvanized tower had rusted here and there, especially on the narrow ladder that went from the bottom to the disintegrated wooden platform used for servicing the mill. Zemo stood looking at the relic and saw a drawing that reflected the past. The Y Diamond had a few windmills still in operation where electricity remained distant, and there were two wells whose pumps were powered by gasoline engines. The Moore Well had not been used in decades but nobody had taken the time to dismantle the tower. Zemo wondered why the Y Diamond hadn't hired a well driller to deepen the old hand dug well and have more water in that section of rangeland.

He walked closer and saw that someone had covered the top of the hole with heavy timbers to prevent animals or humans from falling into the hole. Bayard had told him that the hand dug well went down sixty feet. Zemo tried to imagine the work that had been required to accomplish such a feat as digging the well with a crowbar and shovel.

He decided to draw the windmill from various angles and even attempt to capture its shadows when the sun was right. With arms akimbo he looked back up to the fan. "You are sure some kind of old-timer," he said to the windmill. "I wonder if you're older than Bayard."

The corrals were made *estacada* style with double mesquite posts every four feet with smaller mesquite logs laid horizontally between the posts that were wired together at intervals from two feet above ground to the tops of the posts. Bayard had told Zemo that this type of corral lasted longer than the corrals made from lumber because the lumber was all softwood and tended to rot easily while the mesquite, a definite hardwood, remained intact for many years.

Zemo returned to his pickup, gathered his paper, pens, ink and makeshift easel. He walked back to draw the windmill and corrals. A good-sized boulder with a flat top two feet off the ground served as his chair for one view of the complex. Because of the way the corral was built, the drawing took more time than he anticipated, but he liked the finished product. He took the drawing back to the pickup to put on the table, then returned for another viewpoint of the windmill and corrals. By this time the sun had started to descend to the western horizon so he was able to capture the shadow of the windmill on the ground to the east. It worked out well because the corral's shadow was cast close by without interfering with that of the windmill.

The drawings finished, he propped them up on the far side of the table in the trailer to look at them from a distance. He cocked his head and smiled. "I think I got it," he said aloud. As dusk was approaching quickly, he put the drawings away and prepared his steak supper.

Early the following morning Zemo got everything in order before making his pot of coffee. He wanted to get out to the corrals in time to capture the scene in the early light of morning to get another view of the windmill and corrals. Sipping his coffee, he gathered his drawing materials under one arm. Carrying his coffee cup he walked out to the corrals, wondering how many cattle had watered there over the years and why Henry Moore had sold out instead of trying to accumulate more grazing land.

He wished there was another boulder to sit upon on the side from which he wanted to draw, but it was grassy ground that he sat down on to begin the early morning drawing of shadows. He liked the light and wondered what the corrals and windmill would look like if he used oil paint or watercolors, mediums he had never tried.

A fair sized arroyo nearby had a number of old gnarled mesquite trees lining its banks. He had noticed them the day before. As he finished the drawing of the corral he decided to draw a landscape of the arroyo with its old mesquites standing like markers for the stream bed that ran full of muddy water when there was enough rainfall.

After breakfast he began the arroyo landscape, sitting on an old mesquite log that he had dragged upslope from the arroyo. He decided to make the initial drawing in pencil and draw the ink lines later because there seemed to be a lot more to draw than he was used to. The trees and rocks challenged him to make them look real and not out of place. Up the arroyo near the bank he noticed an old cottonwood trunk that had been uprooted by some long past flood down the arroyo. It caused Zemo to wonder why the old gnarled mesquite hadn't fallen from the dominating force of the same floodwater.

He turned to look back at the windmill and corral and noticed that grasses had filled in where cattle once denuded the landscape near the watering place. "That might be something to add to the other drawings," he said, before beginning to draw the arroyo and its vicinity. The old mesquite trees seemed like groups of guards next to the banks of the arroyo and continuing a short way beyond. He began drawing the trees first, deciding to fill in the arroyo behind them once he finished the trees. The periodic flooding had cut the banks so that the arroyo's channel was now nearly three feet deep. The bed was sand and fine gravel with occasional rocks and a few boulders that had made their way downward, pushed by flowing water when it flooded the arroyo.

Zemo worked diligently drawing the mesquite trees and became so engrossed in their various shapes with twists and turns that he didn't hear the horse and rider approach. When he finally leaned back to look at what he had accomplished he jumped when he heard a female voice behind him say "Hi, I didn't want to interrupt you so I stayed back here."

Zemo turned to face his visitor. He saw an auburn-haired girl with a Stetson on her head at a slight tilt. He put his drawing equipment on the ground and stood up. "Hello," he said. "I'm Zemo Doyle."

"I know, my father told me all about you. I'm Maggie Landers, Jim's daughter."

"I recognize Jim's roan gelding," Zemo said, walking toward Maggie. "Why don't you put Old Roany in the corral and I'll heat up some coffee."

"That sounds like just what I could use after the two-hour ride out here from headquarters. I'm not used to riding after three years in art school."

Maggie rode the roan into the corral and closed the rickety pole gate, fastening it shut with a piece of rusty baling wire. Then she followed Zemo who had gone to the trailer to light the little propane stove with its two burners. Maggie stood at the door.

"Come on in and sit down," Zemo said. "The coffee should heat up in a few minutes."

Maggie entered the trailer and sat at the table watching Zemo as he waited for the coffee to begin simmering.

"Dad showed me the portrait you drew of him. You are really very good."

"Thank you," Zemo replied looking back at the coffee pot.

"Where did you go to art school?" she asked.

"I never went to art school, I just started drawing in grade school and one of my teachers knew about art and encouraged me to continue. I did for a while but quit to be a cowboy, but that didn't last long."

"Dad told me you used to work here for the Y Diamond and then quit to go off rodeoing. Do you still ride bareback broncs?"

"No. I figured I can make a better living drawing since there is a gallery man in Yuma who likes what I do."

"That's smart," Maggie said as Zemo poured the coffee. "I have never seen anyone make a pleasant living riding broncs in rodeos. Dad said he would give you your job back at the Y Diamond anytime you want it."

Zemo put the coffee mugs on the table. "There's sugar in that bowl," he said pointing to the small bowl with a top covering the contents. "Your father told me that, too but I feel the need to keep drawing. It seems like a part of me. I am glad I have been able to make a living from it so far."

"That's a question I have about my art," Maggie said, and took off her Stetson so that her hair fell down around her shoulders.

"What's that?" Zemo asked.

"Whether I will be able to live from it or be forced to get a day job," Maggie said as she stirred a teaspoon of sugar into her coffee.

Zemo took the drawings that he had made so far at the Y Diamond and handed them to Maggie. She looked at them carefully and went through the pile twice before saying anything.

"I can see why you are selling your art, Zemo. This is fine work. You have what it takes. That's for sure."

Zemo couldn't keep from staring across the table at Maggie. He found her fascinating. She wasn't what one would call beautiful like Alicia. The small freckles on her somewhat turned up nose between her sparkling green eyes gave her a look of someone who had the confidence it took to try making a living with her art. Zemo's eyes dropped and took in her upper figure and he found her well proportioned and wondered what the breasts that stretched her shirt looked like.

"I must say, Zemo, you are really giving me the once over," Maggie said impishly.

"I've never been with a girl like you before," he said, and looked back into her eyes.

"I'm just me, Maggie."

"But you're interesting to talk to and I enjoy listening to what you have to say about art. I also enjoy looking at you," Zemo said, knowing that she wouldn't panic over his compliments.

"I think you are special, too," Maggie said. "There are not many cowboys who would decide to hang up their spurs and try drawing without going to art school."

"Would you like some lunch?" Zemo asked.

"I brought some with me. Are you ready to eat already?"

"Not really, I just thought I would ask so I could start something on the stove for you."

"Come to think of it, I had better go get my lunch out of Dad's saddle bags or it might cook and I don't care much for soggy bread."

Maggie rose and went out the trailer door. Zemo followed her up to the corral. She undid the baling wire on the old gate, went up to the roan, opened the left saddlebag and took out a folded over brown paper sack bulging with contents. "My mother always packs too much lunch. Perhaps we can share?"

"Fine with me if it's OK with you, Maggie."

"Good. That's settled. I'll take it back to the trailer."

"I'll wait here," Zemo said. "I just had an idea that might turn into something good on paper."

Maggie trudged back to the trailer and soon reappeared by Zemo's side as he gazed into the corral. "Are you ready to tell me your idea?" She asked.

"I am thinking about drawing this old corral and windmill with longhorn cattle inside it like they once were. I suppose it's a dream or something like it. I always wonder if the olden times weren't better than now."

"I have wondered that, too. But, I have read enough about that early history to know, as someone said, 'It was tough on horses and mules and downright hell on women.' There was the romance that probably attracts us now because we didn't have to live during those tough times."

"I haven't read as much as you have but I agree with what you're saying," Zemo said. "I just think that putting longhorns in a drawing of that corral might be nice to do just for the hell of it."

"Let's talk about it over lunch," Maggie suggested.

They returned to the trailer where Maggie gave Zemo a sandwich and Zemo heated coffee for both of them. Again, sitting opposite Maggie at the table he had trouble keeping his eyes away from her. He couldn't quite put his finger on why she intrigued him, but there was no doubt in his mind that he had met a unique woman.

After finishing half their sandwiches, Zemo put his back on the plate. "I would like to draw your portrait, Maggie," he said looking into her eyes while he chewed the bite of sandwich.

"Why in the world would you want to draw me, Zemo?"

"Because I think you are the most interesting woman I have ever known. You have a certain look I have never seen before and to me it is an honest look that I really appreciate."

"Wow, nobody ever told me that before," Maggie said. "In fact not many boys ever wanted to talk to me at all."

"Their loss," Zemo said. "In my eyes I find you beautiful and I would like to try to capture that beauty in a drawing."

"I suppose we had better get started when we finish lunch because I need at least two hours to ride back to headquarters."

Zemo took his drawing things back to the corral, asked Maggie to sit in the grass near the boulder he had sat on to draw his first picture of the windmill. "I would like one with your hat on and one without," he said. " And I like the tilt that you had with the hat when you rode in."

Maggie sat down and posed for the portrait. Zemo worked quickly but surely as he drew her face and bust. Carefully he put the finishing touches on the drawing, and then held it up for her to see.

"That is really good, Zemo," she said. "You made me look beautiful."

"That was easy. You are beautiful, Maggie."

"I don't know what to say," she said.

"You don't have to say anything. Let's go into the corral for the one with your Stetson on. I think if you stand next to the roan I can include part of him also in the idea I have for this portrait."

They entered the corral where the roan stood patiently next to the old mesquite poles. Maggie walked over and stood next to him with her hand gripping the saddle horn.

"That's exactly how I had planned to ask you to pose," Zemo said. "If you will look toward the old windmill, I can get a nice partial profile for this one. I like your profile, too."

Maggie looked up at the old dilapidated windmill and Zemo went to work on the drawing. Midway through Maggie turned toward Zemo.

"Sorry I had to look away from the pose, but I want to ask you if I can come back tomorrow with my paints and do a portrait of you."

"I'd like that, just to have you come back tomorrow," Zemo said, and then looked back at the drawing because he felt the heat of his blush spread over his face.

Maggie smiled impishly before Zemo felt ready to look at her again. Then she returned to the pose looking at the windmill. "I'll ride out earlier because I like to ponder over my painting and your portrait might take a few hours. You won't have to sit still all day because I will need some breaks also."

"Maybe I can draw you while you paint me," Zemo offered.

"That might be a great way to do it. I do like your look when you raise your right eyebrow when you are thinking about something like what to reply to a question."

"You seem to notice a lot about me," Zemo said.

"I guess that's what getting acquainted is all about," she said.

About a half hour later Zemo stepped back to look at the drawing. "Finished except for some small additions I might make this evening while I am waiting for supper to cook."

"What are you going to cook?"

"I've got some beans soaking and I'll cook them and a beefsteak."

"I wish I could stay for supper," Maggie said.

"That would be nice," Zemo said, and paused. "Tilt your head just a bit higher so I can get the brim of your Stetson right."

Maggie shifted her position and tilted her head so the hat brim wouldn't cover her face.

"Perfect, Zemo said. "Not much more, just have to get that brim right and then a few touches here and there."

"Just in time," Maggie said. "I had better start for home. Thanks for a wonderful day, Zemo. What a pleasure to meet a fellow artist."

"I enjoyed it, too. I hope you like the portraits when I get them touched up," Zemo said.

"I already like them. This one is extra special. I'll see you early tomorrow so I can paint your portrait."

"I am happy to meet you, Maggie. Have a good ride home."

Zemo took the portrait and his equipment back to the trailer and began boiling his beans. He sat at the table gazing toward the trail back to the Y Diamond and wished he were riding with Maggie. He scrutinized the two portraits and determined what he would do to finish them after he finished supper.

The beans almost boiled dry while he walked around outside the trailer thinking about Maggie and wondering what might happen the following day. He barely saved the beans and then fried a steak to go with them. Cleaning up after supper he returned to walk outside until sunset. He didn't try to get Maggie off his mind. He enjoyed pondering what it might be like to take her into his arms and feel her body next to his and kiss her.

A beautiful sunrise with a few long clouds greeted Zemo when he stepped out of the trailer. He looked at the reddish orange glow on the old mesquite corral and imagined how it would look painted instead of just done with pen and ink or pencil. He looked forward to Maggie's arrival and to watch how she did her art. But, most of all he just wanted her presence.

Zemo was standing under the windmill tower when she rode up and put the roan gelding into the corral. "Good morning," he said, over the poles. You must have started early to get out here so soon."

"I got up even before Dad, got my stuff together, grabbed a bite of breakfast, saddled Roany and away we went. Good morning to you, too. I saw you looking up at the windmill as I rode in."

"I'm thinking about climbing that ladder and perching on the platform to draw the corral full of longhorns."

"That platform doesn't look too sturdy from here," she said.

"I think you're right. That's why I was looking it over before I started climbing. The ladder is pretty well rusted out so I probably ought to imagine I'm up there rather than take a chance on the whole thing collapsing with me up on top."

"That makes sense to me," she said, unloading her painting paraphernalia from the saddlebags.

Zemo watched Maggie arrange her brushes, paint and water near the boulder he had sat on previously. "It will take a little while for me to get all this organized because I haven't used my paints since I left California." A little while later she said, "Why don't you stand by the corral where I was yesterday? I like the way the light hits those poles."

"I liked that place for the light also," Zemo said, and walked over to the corral.

"Get in a comfortable position, because my portrait of you will take longer than your picture of me," Maggie said.

Zemo leaned against the corral fence and put his arm over the top pole. "Is this all right?" he asked.

"Look over my left shouilder."

Zemo turned his head and focused on a small tree in the background.

"That's fine," Maggie said. "Are you comfortable?"

"Right now, I'm fine."

"All right I'm going to go for it," she said and began to paint.

The corral had sunk through the years, and since its abandonment nobody had done any repairs on it. Zemo tried to picture the old structure when it was new fifty or sixty years before. He stood patiently while Maggie painted and tried to imagine the longhorns milling around inside the corral. He had seen Goodman's longhorns and remembered the multi-colored animals. Again the thought of painting them with color piqued his interest. He remembered a big freckled faced bull with brown ears and splotches of black and brown on his sides and down his back. He thought, perhaps, that a single animal, challenging the world in the corral, would be a portrait rather than just another cattle scene. He remembered enough of the bull to draw him easily. Painting him with watercolor was another thing he would have to ask Maggie about once she finished.

Maggie washed the brushes she had been using and covered her paints. Holding the portrait with Zemo's face accomplished, she held it out to study. Then she laid it down beside the paints and walked up to where Zemo still held his pose. She abruptly kissed him on his left cheek. Zemo's eyes grew large with surprise.

"I hope you don't think I am too forward," Maggie said and smiled at him.

Zemo turned and looked her straight in her eyes and without answering her, took her shoulders into his hands and pulled her toward him. Wrapping his arms around her waist and back, he kissed her. It wasn't a peck on the cheek, but a passionate kiss on her lips to which she surrendered. He knew that she felt the same about him as he did about her.

After the kiss he kept holding her and looking into her eyes as he smiled lovingly at her. Maggie initiated the next kiss and they remained in that embrace for several minutes before she pushed him gently an arm length away. "I think I had better get back to painting, Zemo," she said, tilting her head impishly.

"I expect you're right, Maggie, but I sure enjoyed that time in between."

"Me, too," she replied.

She returned to her painting and finished Zemo's portrait in a half hour. Holding it up for him to see, she asked, "Zemo, do you like it?"

Zemo tilted his head as he looked at her work. "You are very good with those watercolors, Maggie. I like the portrait very much. Do I really have that look in my eyes?"

"That's what I saw," she said.

"Will you teach me about watercolors?"

"I can show you the basics about colors and so forth, but with your talent for drawing I would say you can develop your own brush stroke style."

"When do we begin the lessons?" he asked.

"How about tomorrow? That is, if tomorrow is all right with you."

"I'll need to go to town and buy some paints and brushes," he said.

"You can use mine. In fact, by the time I get back to headquarters it will be too late to paint anything so I'll leave all this stuff here with you. You can practice this evening and tomorrow morning."

"That should be fun," he said. "It will also take my mind off wanting to kiss you again."

"Zemo, you are something," she said. "Let's take this stuff to your trailer so I can get on that roan and head for home."

"I was hoping you'd stay for supper," he said.

"And then it would be too dark to ride back to headquarters. My father would be out here a half hour after sundown if I wasn't back by then."

"I know all that, Maggie. I would just enjoy having supper with you."

"Maybe before I have to go back to California I can borrow Dad's pickup and drive out here for supper," she said.

"That would suit me fine. By the way, when do you have to go back to California?"

"I still have another week of vacation," she said. "Will you write to me?"

"I sure will even though I don't get into town much to mail letters."

"How long do you think you'll stay here at the ranch?" she asked. "I can send letters to you here."

"It's hard telling how long I'll stay around here. It might be a month or it might be two weeks. It all depends on how much I get done to take to Yuma."

"I'll just send my letters to you here until you tell me to send them elsewhere. I'll write out my address in Santa Barbara and bring it tomorrow."

"Where is Santa Barbara?" Zemo asked.

"It's a hundred miles north of Los Angeles on the coast. It's a pretty place and there's a lot to paint there. For this last semester I will be painting mostly because I have finished the class work."

"Are you coming for supper tomorrow?"

"It depends on if I can borrow Dad's pickup. Right now I had better saddle up and scram home," she said, and gave Zemo a short kiss. "See you in the morning."

Zemo carried the art materials back to the trailer and put them on the table. Then he stepped outside again to wave good-bye to Maggie.

After pouring himself a cup of coffee, he sat down and began painting with Maggie's watercolors to try this new medium. At first the brush felt awkward, but he didn't try to paint anything in particular. He just wanted to see how the brush worked on the paper. He continued after supper and into the night working by the light of his kerosene lamp. The more he worked with the brush the more confident he became. Once he grew sleepy he cleaned up the brush and covered the paints so they wouldn't dry up overnight. As he prepared for bed he looked forward to seeing Maggie in the morning. As he closed his eyes there was a smile on his face.

The following morning Zemo opened the watercolors again and began painting the old corral with a single longhorn bull standing in the middle of it looking through the gate as if he was trying to decide to crash through it. He had begun by experimenting with mixing the various colors to see what they produced. That way he found the right combinations to capture the color of the corral and the surrounding landscape as well as what he imagined the old bull would have looked like. He became so engrossed in his work that he didn't realize Maggie had not ridden up.

First he heard the sound of a vehicle and looked away from his painting to see a white pickup he recognized as belonging to Jim Landers. He looked up at the sun to estimate the time. As the truck came closer he saw Maggie in her Stetson behind the steering wheel. After rinsing the paintbrush, he put it down and waved to her.

She drove up to the corral, parked, turned off the engine and stepped out. "Hey, Zemo, I can stay for supper and even brought some steaks for us."

"Wonderful," he said. "Come here and look at my corral painting."

Maggie walked over to where Zemo had been working and looked at his progress. "You don't need any lessons from me," she said. "This is really good."

"Are you just saying that?" Zemo asked.

"No, dear man, how in the world do you understand color so well?"

"I really don't understand color except I try to match it up to what I'm painting."

"I doubt if I can give you any lessons," Maggie said, and sighed.

"Are you talking about painting?" He asked.

She caught on immediately. "Zemo, I think I should tell you that I am an inexperienced woman."

"When we get around to all that, it might be interesting because I am probably at your same level."

When they stopped laughing Zemo and Maggie put their arms around each other and enjoyed the tenderness of their kisses. After Zemo resumed painting he began with the pattern of color on the longhorn bull. Maggie watched, mostly in silence as he worked intently. When he was satisfied he washed the brushes and handed the watercolors to Maggie.

"Your turn," he said. "What are you going to paint?"

"I haven't given that much thought," she said. "I've been enjoying watching you too much. I suppose I could do another portrait of you looking over the corral at the bull that isn't there."

Zemo walked over and took a comfortable pose by the corral pretending he was looking at something inside the enclosure. Maggie opened the paints again and started Zemo's portrait. When she finished, Zemo suggested they take a break for some lunch. Later that afternoon Zemo gathered mesquite wood.

Maggie closed up her paints and handed them to Zemo after he got the mesquite fire started. "I'm going into town with Dad tomorrow. Go ahead and use my paints if you want to."

"Thanks, I have a painting in mind I would like to try from memory when we were gathering. I am thinking about a painting showing the cattle walking along from the point of view of the man on horseback driving them from the rear."

"That sounds like quite a project. While I'm in town would you like to have me buy you some watercolor paints and paper?"

"That would be really nice of you, Maggie. I'll give you some money. How much do you figure all that will cost?"

"It shouldn't run over twenty," she said.

Zemo reached into his Levis and extracted a roll of bills from which he peeled off a twenty-dollar bill and handed it to her.

"I'll ask Dad for the pickup day after tomorrow so I can bring the stuff out here to you. He mentioned he was going to ride with your uncle to check on a fence crew he has working on the boundary fence between the Quarter Circle V and us. He said that Goodman fellow is getting desperate for range and has cut the fence too many times."

"I remember working that country with Uncle Bayard when I was here before. I also had a set to with Goodman at The Silver Dollar Saloon."

"Dad didn't tell me about that," she said.

"I never told him about it."

"There must be a lot I don't know about you," she said, raising her left eyebrow and smiling.

"There's probably a lot I don't know about you, too. Like you said before, that's what getting acquainted is all about."

After supper they sat at the table and talked about themselves. Zemo told Maggie how he had wanted to become a cowboy and then changed his mind after seeing his uncle seeming stagnate in his job. Maggie explained how she went to art school in Santa Barbara to learn how to live away from her parents even though she loved them dearly.

"I just hope I can make a living with art," she said.

"So far, I've done better selling art than being either a cowboy or a bronc rider in rodeos."

Just before sunset they kissed each other goodnight and stood holding one another closely for a few minutes. "I like getting to know you, Zemo," she said.

"It won't be the same here without you."

"I almost forgot," she said breaking away and reaching into her back pocket of her Levis. She handed him a piece of paper. "This is my address in Santa Barbara so you can write to me."

Zemo took the paper, looked at the writing on it and stuffed it into his shirt pocket. "I have never written a letter in my life," he said.

"It's time you did," she said. "I'll get some envelopes and writing paper along with the paints."

After Maggie had driven off Zemo stood gazing at the dust from the pickup. He thought about how different he felt about Maggie than he had about Alicia. There was preciousness about Maggie that he never found in Alicia. He wondered if he would have felt the same toward Alicia had he not gone off to the rodeo.

He returned to the trailer, took out a sheet of paper and began a pencil drawing of a herd of driven cattle. Ahead of the herd he drew his uncle riding "point". For a moment he stood back and scrutinized his drawing. With deliberation he grabbed his eraser and began modifying the cattle. Instead of modern European cattle that roamed the ranges of the Y Diamond, he began putting long horns on the critters like Big Joe Goodman had next door. He also drew the patterns where the multi colors on the hides would show up in the painting once he began painting the watercolors onto the picture. When he had the pencil work done he could barely keep his eyes open so the night swallowed him into sleep.

The following day he began with the watercolors and found it fascinating to make different shades to use on the hide patterns of the cattle. Around noon he stopped painting and realized he missed seeing Maggie. He heated some beans and filled the void in his stomach, but he couldn't get Maggie out of his mind. He thought about driving his rig back to headquarters, but thought better of that idea because she had gone to town with her father. He finished the beans and returned to the watercolor hoping to finish it by nightfall so Maggie could see it in the morning when she arrived with his paints and paper.

Just as the sun raced toward the horizon behind the mountains to the west of the old waterhole he stood back to assess his work. He particularly liked the way he had placed one longhorn looking toward the rear of the herd without stopping. It almost looked like the critter was looking for some way to escape the herd.

Maggie arrived next morning in the pickup again shortly after breakfast. Zemo rushed out of the trailer to welcome her. She carried two packages toward the trailer.

"I sure missed seeing you yesterday," Zemo blurted.

"I missed you, too, but I had a good time in town with Dad. He was glad I went with him because I haven't seen much of him on this vacation."

"I wonder why not," Zemo said, and smiled.

Maggie handed Zemo the packages. He turned and took them into the trailer after inviting her in for coffee. Seated at the table they looked at each other almost as if they hadn't seen one another in a month instead of just a day.

"I had lunch at The Zorro Café," Maggie said.

"I used to go in there," Zemo said, thinking about walking Alicia home when she got off work.

"I found that out from Alicia Quiroz," Maggie said. "She and I graduated from high school together and are still good friends. I told her about meeting you and she said you had walked her home a few times but had gone off to ride in rodeos."

"Yeah, I walked her home a few times and thought she was quite beautiful."

"She told me about running off with a Mexican rancher and getting married. That was not a pleasant story. It seems that this man beat her up a few times after she got pregnant so she ran away and came back to Rinconada."

"I heard from Frank Spencer that she ran off with a Mexican rancher. Is she all right?"

"Sure, Alicia is a survivor. All her bruises have disappeared but she is showing her condition. Were you in love with Alicia, Zemo?"

"I thought I was, but I reckon I was more in love with being a bronc rider. When I got back from Yuma after doing all that drawing she was gone."

"Do you want to see her again?"

"No, Maggie. Not any more than just as a friend. I was more in lust than in love. After meeting you I now know what love really is."

"Are you telling me you love me?"

"I reckon."

She got up from the table, stepped over to where Zemo sat and slid in next to him. "I love you, too, Zemo Doyle. I really do."

She put her arms around him and kissed him. "Alicia was stupid not to wait for you. She wasn't too smart in school either.

"I think I finished the cattle drive painting," Zemo said. "Let me out so I can get it for you to critique."

He went over to the box in which he kept his finished work and took the watercolor of the cattle herd out and held it up for her to look at. "I sketched it in pencil first," he said.

"Wow, I can't even see any pencil marks."

"I got used to watercolors quickly. I remember using them in school but these are different."

"Things have improved since you had watercolors in school. This is a fine piece of work. The cattle seem alive and I love that one old wooly-headed critter that is looking back to see if there are any cowboys. I also like the perspective where you are looking down on their backs."

"Well, I have seen this view a few times right here on the Y Diamond."

"Open your packages and see what I bought with your twenty bucks."

He opened the larger package first and looked at the tubes of watercolors and brushes. She had included a sealed package of watercolor paper and a set of small containers with covers in which he could keep his paint moist. "Did you have enough money?"

"I even brought you two dollars change," she said reaching into her Levi pocket. She handed him the two one-dollar bills. Unwrap the other package and see if you like the writing paper."

Zemo undid the string around the wrapping paper and opened the box of stationery.

"I figured you had enough pens and ink already," she said. "Now you won't have any excuses not to write me letters when I'm in Santa Barbara."

"When do you have to leave?"

"In three days I have to catch the train. It's an overnight trip to Los Angeles and then I take the bus to Santa Barbara. There's a train but I would have to wait most of the day for it to leave. For some reason north-south and east-west schedules don't match up well at all."

"If I didn't have all these paintings and drawings to do for Oliphant I would offer to drive you over there."

"That would be fun, but I don't expect that. You have your work cut out with your art."

"I expect you're right on that score. I need to get a bunch done while he is buying."

"I'll have to get busy very soon and learn how to market my art if I want to make a living at it."

The night before she was to leave for California Maggie rode back to headquarters in time to reach home before dark. She and Zemo had said their good-byes in between her tears. As she disappeared beyond the hills Zemo went back into the trailer and wrote his first letter to her. He also thought about moving to another ranch for some different scenery and buildings. He knew one ranch closer to Rinconada that had a former Butterfield stage station on it. He thought that might make a good painting even though it was in disrepair. There was an old adobe ranch house with a wide territorial style porch nearby that had tall eucalyptus trees surrounding it. Somehow the old waterhole wouldn't be the same without Maggie's visits.

Before he got ready to leave the next day, his uncle rode up and they drank what was left in the coffee pot. Zemo enjoyed seeing Bayard and showed him the trail drive painting in which Bayard was riding "point".

"By gollies, I didn't know you were such an artist, Nephew. Jim Landers told me you did pretty well out there in Yuma selling stuff to some gallery."

"I have a lot to do before I go back there," Zemo said. I'll stop by before I leave again for Yuma."

"I'd like that," Bayard said, taking off his Stetson and scratching the top of his head. "I'd better get moving along and check on those fence builders. I wish there was some way to build a tall stone wall to keep that varmint Goodman from cuttin' wire."

"It might be cheaper to hire a guard to ride fence all the time over there," Zemo said.

"Big Joe will shoot his mouth off one of these days and we won't have to worry about him anymore."

Bayard rode off toward the boundary fence while Zemo finished putting his gear in order in the trailer. He gathered some mesquite wood and wrapped a pile of it with baling wire before lifting it into the bed of the pickup. "Never know if there's any wood when you get somewhere, so it's best to carry some along," he said to the pile.

As he drove through headquarters Zemo noticed that Jim Lander's pickup was gone so he assumed that Maggie was in Rinconada boarding her train to California. He headed in the opposite direction to the small village of Pinnacle situated at the northern base of the mountains in oak country. He parked in front of the grocery store and went in to buy a few supplies for the week he planned to stay around the place. He had once ridden through on the Y Diamond gather looking for strays, but he remembered it enough to want to draw some of the buildings. He also wanted to try his watercolors on paintings of the oak woodlands with their under story of tall grasses that would become green again once the summer storms began.

After getting his supplies Zemo drove back and forth through the village looking at the buildings and the few people who ogled at his presence in the pickup and camper. He remembered what Bayard had told him about Pinnacle being a community serving a few scattered mines and cattle ranches. He spotted one establishment that announced its business with a battered sign, "WELDING". The grocery store was really a general store. He had noticed all sorts of things hanging from the ceiling and propped against the adobe walls. He had wondered how long the store had been in Pinnacle and if it might have been the first business to start there. He drove back to the small parking space in front of McDaniels Groceries, stopped the pickup and began drawing the building. It interested him that all the while he was parked in front of the place there had been no customer enter. He began to wonder if the populace of Pinnacle didn't buy at the local store and drove all the way into Rinconada instead. His questions were answered just after he finished the drawing when a battered car sputtered up and two men with hard hats got out to enter McDaniels. They left the car with its motor running. Zemo looked up as they returned to the car with two six-packs of beer each.

Zemo thought about that situation and wondered if there would be enough money left for groceries by the end of the week. The men backed the old Studebaker onto the main road in town and the driver shifted into first, grinding the gears.

Next on Zemo's list was the welding shop, but he wanted to include someone working on something. However, as he drove up to the building, a man was closing the large garage doors for the day. Across a dirt road from the general store he had seen a building when he had ridden through before. It was not just a typical plastered whitewashed adobe, there was also a small sign that said "Pinnacle Inn". Zemo decided to investigate. Parking outside in an ample lot, he stepped out of the pickup and went up to the entrance. He pulled open the heavy wooden door and walked into the place where the darkness made him hesitate until his eyes got used to it. Glancing around he saw a few tables with rustic wooden chairs and in a side room he spotted a bar where a Mexican man stood behind the plank top polishing glasses.

"Come in, Señor," the man said, and placed the glass with others stacked on a shelf behind the bar.

Zemo went into the room with the bar and sat on one of eight barstools. The bartender put his hands on the inside of the bar and looked at Zemo as if he were trying to recognize him.

"What can I get you?" the bartender asked.

""I'd like a tequila straight," Zemo replied.

The bartender took a shot glass from the shelf behind, grabbed a bottle labeled "Sauza" and filled the shot glass almost to the top. "Lime and salt?"

"No thanks," Zemo said. "I like the taste as it comes out of the bottle."

Zemo took half the tequila in one long sip.

"Do you work around here?" the bartender asked.

"Not now," Zemo answered. "I used to work with the Y Diamond but I am an artist now."

"I know Jim Landers from the Y Diamond," the bartender said.

"I guess everyone in the valley knows Jim. He's been at that ranch for a long time."

"Don Boyd, the owner of the Inn is a good friend with Jim Landers. He also owns the Bar O over next to the canyon. If you eat a steak here it came from Mister Boyd's ranch."

"I'll have to come back and try that. I would also like to come back tomorrow and draw some pictures of this place."

"I open up at ten in the morning in case there's a thirsty miner or cowboy. The cook, who is also the waiter, gets here at eleven in case there is someone who wants a steak at noon."

"That sounds good. I can start with the outside and then when you arrive I can do the interior, including you."

Zemo finished the tequila.

The bartender grabbed the bottle again. "*Otro*?"

"I might as well, I can't dance when there's no music," Zemo said and smiled.

"If you come in on Saturday night, Mister Boyd will be here playing his guitar and singing. He knows more Mexican songs than I do."

"That sounds great. I'll try to make it back Saturday," Zemo said, and sipped his tequila. "By the way, I'm Zemo Doyle."

The bartender extended his hand and shook Zemo's. "They call me Pepe. My last name is Salas."

"Were you born here in Pinnacle?" Zemo asked.

"I sure was. It will be twenty-five years ago next Wednesday."

"Happy birthday."

"*Gracias.*"

"Do you know a good place for me to pull off the road with my camp trailer?"

"If you drive to the west end of town and take the dirt road to the right for a mile there is an old barn sitting out in the middle of nowhere. The property belongs to my family. The barnyard is level and should be fine for your trailer."

"Thanks, Pepe. That helps a lot. I reckon since I don't have to go searching for a place I can have one more tequila."

Pepe poured another tequila for Zemo.

"What do I owe you?" Zemo asked.

"A dollar twenty."

Zemo took two dollars from his pocket and placed it on the bar. Pepe reached across to take the money to the cash register.

"The change is yours, Pepe.'

"Gracias."

Zemo downed the shot of tequila, slid off the barstool and waved at Pepe as he headed for the door.

"*Adios,* Señor Doyle. Enjoy our old barnyard."

"Thanks, Pepe, I'll see you in the morning."

Following Pepe's simple directions Zemo found the Salas barn, parked his rig on the most level ground he could see and prepared his supper. As he arrived he knew he had to paint the old adobe structure with old weathered gray gables and doors that hung from their bottom hinges and were partly buried in the sand and dirt that had blown in over the years.

As the sun plunged toward the horizon he quickly finished his supper and took out his sketchpad and pens and ink. Sitting on the doorstep of the trailer he had a perfect view of the barn so that he could capture the doors and the sides that had been eroded in spite of the slightly overhanging roof. He finished the drawing in an hour just as darkness began invading the oak woodland landscape. Early the following morning he painted the barn in watercolors and concluded that the color brought the old structure back to life yet showed its history.

Arriving at The Pinnacle Inn at 9:00 o'clock he began a watercolor painting of the building and by the time Pepe came to open the Inn he had made a good start. After putting the painting away, he went in with his equipment to paint the interior while Pepe did his morning cleanup. Zemo greeted the bartender and sat at one of the tables to get a panoramic view of the bar and lounge area.

The place was empty of customers when he began, but just as he was ready to do a portrait of Pepe, a grizzled miner arrived for a glass of wine. Zemo continued with the painting and managed to include Pepe standing behind the bar leaning on his hands while talking in Spanish with the old miner. The miner drank four glasses of wine before putting his money on the bar and leaving.

"That was Alfonso Zepeda," Pepe said. "He has been digging into the mountain almost all his life, always hoping for the big vein. He has always managed to make enough to live on, and the wine seems to give him energy somehow."

"At least he has some enjoyment besides his pick and shovel," Zemo said.

"He never married so his only companions have been burros. He is one of the old timers around Pinnacle."

Zemo continued the portrait of Pepe until he was happy with the results. "Take a look and see if you recognize yourself," he said.

Pepe looked at the painting with wide eyes. "Wow, that is really good. Nobody ever made a picture of me before."

"If you can hold still and nobody comes in for a drink, I'll do another and give it to you."

Pepe stood almost motionless behind the bar as Zemo worked on the second portrait. A cowboy wearing spurs entered, sat on a barstool and ordered an A1 beer. Zemo stopped Pepe's portrait and began to paint the cowboy sitting on the barstool with his spurs on.

After two beers the cowboy slid off the barstool and ambled out the door. Zemo had finished enough of the painting so that he did the rest from memory.

Pepe liked the portrait and thanked Zemo profusely for the gift. "Are you coming in tomorrow to listen to Mister Boyd?" he asked, as Zemo was packing up his paints, brushes and paper.

"I hope to," Zemo said. "I have a couple more subjects I want to paint before I leave for The Zopilote Ranch to paint the old Butterfield Stage Station."

Zemo arrived at The Pinnacle Inn in the early evening on Saturday. Pepe introduced him to Don Boyd and Zemo immediately asked his permission to paint his portrait while he was playing.

"Sure, go ahead, Zemo," Boyd said. "Just make sure you make me handsome."

Zemo hustled out to his rig, grabbed his painting stuff and returned to the bar where Boyd had begun playing his guitar and singing. The place had not become crowded so Zemo had an ample opportunity to capture Boyd's essence as he played and sang. Zemo consumed three tequilas as he worked and never felt a bit drunk. He liked Boyd's expensive Stetson that he had shaped to go with his six-foot frame which he had covered with a buckskin jacket and faded blue Levis. His boots were obviously custom-made with six rows of stitching on the tops.

People began showing up after seven o'clock and the tables and barstools were filled by eight. Pepe kept busy filling drink orders. In between songs Boyd told humorous ranch stories that delighted the crowd even though, as Zemo felt, they had all heard the stories several times over through the years. Zemo looked around into the dining room and saw that all the tables had customers. He marveled that way out here in a small hamlet one man singing and playing a guitar could fill a restaurant even though Pepe had told him that The Pinnacle Inn steaks were well known as far as Rinconada. He had also mentioned that the dudes who came from the east to the guest ranches all knew about Don Boyd's establishment.

Boyd came over to Zemo's table during one of his breaks and looked at the finished portrait. "You're pretty good, cowboy. Why don't you try selling your art work?"

Zemo hesitated. "I'll give it a try one of these days," he said.

Underneath, Zemo wanted to keep the portrait of Don Boyd to sell to Chauncey Oliphant when he got to Yuma. He felt that it would round out the collection quite well. He was glad that the bartender had not told Boyd of the second portrait of Pepe that Zemo had given him. Zemo had had enough tequila and wanted to get back to the Salas barn for a night's sleep.

The following morning he realized it was Sunday and Jim Landers would more than likely be home. He wanted to see if he had a letter from Maggie. He pulled out of Pinnacle early and when he arrived at the Y Diamond he found Landers still enjoying breakfast. Jim invited Zemo to stay and gave him two letters that had arrived from Maggie. Zemo didn't open them until he had left for The Zopilote Ranch to the south, about half way to Rinconada. He pulled off the highway and read what Maggie had written. He had asked Jim to forward any more letters to him at General Delivery in Yuma.

The Butterfield Stage Station picture became part of the collection. Zemo also made a watercolor of the old Zopilote ranch house with the tall eucalyptus trees surrounding it. The ranch owner gave him permission to park near his headquarter corrals for the two nights he was there. The first evening after supper he wrote a long letter to Maggie telling her all about his travels to Pinnacle and elsewhere. He tried to answer her letters as closely as he could. He mailed it in Rinconada and headed west resisting the temptation to stop at The Zorro Café to see what a pregnant Alicia looked like. He felt good about not stopping because he knew in his heart that Maggie was more his type of woman than Alicia Quiroz.

As he drove over the highway toward Yuma he thought about the artwork he had accomplished and hoped that Chauncey Oliphant felt the same way. The closer he came to Yuma the hotter it was in the cab of his pickup. He had seen the evaporative coolers that were installed on the passenger side window of automobiles and thought about getting one for the pickup should he remain around the Yuma desert country for any length of time. He couldn't understand why anyone would live in a place like Yuma where the summer heat was always blistering hot except after a rain. But it rarely rained in Yuma.

As he passed through Wellton he again saw the Wellton-Mohawk irrigation project that gave World War II veterans a chance to homestead the desert and farm it with water from the Colorado River. He thought that farming in such a hot climate would be more than miserable, but the canals and cleared ground made him wonder about how far men would go to make a living. Zemo kept his eyes on the highway as he neared Yuma. After the Marine Base he made the long turn that guided the traffic onto the main road into town.

Parking in front of Arte Place he shut off the engine and opened the door. Before he got out he saw something had changed. The sign "Arte Place was no longer in the front window and behind that window the building looked vacant. Zemo left the pickup and walked across the sidewalk to have a look. He stood with his arms akimbo when he noticed the "For Rent" sign in the small window in the front door.

"What in hell happened here?" he asked the building.

Since it was too late for the River Bank to be open, he decided to go to the Scorpion Bar to see if Henry Montgomery was still there sipping his after-work drink. Parking a half block away from the Scorpion he locked the pickup's cab and went to the bar.

Henry was sitting on his favorite barstool with a drink in front of him. Zemo approached him. "Mister Montgomery, I am glad I found you," he said.

Montgomery turned to see who was talking to him. "Well, hello Zemo. I didn't expect to see you in town again."

"I came to deliver a picture collection I've been working on to Chauncey Oliphant, but when I drove up I saw that the gallery is vacant and for rent. Did he move somewhere else?"

"Zemo, I have some sad news for you, but I would rather you came to the bank in the morning. This bar is no place for our conversation about Chauncey."

"What time in the morning?" Zemo asked.

"I'll come in early around eight o'clock and open up. We can be alone to talk about Chauncey at that time because the two tellers don't arrive until nine."

"I'll see you at the bank at eight sharp," Zemo said, hoping that the banker wasn't too drunk to remember the appointment the next day.

Zemo left the Scorpion after buying a pint bottle of tequila and drove to a spot next to the Colorado River where he found some picnic tables and rest rooms. He prepared his supper and sat on the bench with a glass of tequila wondering what had happened that Montgomery considered sad news and not the kind of topic one would converse about in The Scorpion. He sipped his tequila slowly as he pondered. As the hot Yuma sun sank below the horizon he finished the bottle and contemplated what he wanted to draw in Yuma before he left for California to visit Maggie. Then by the light of his kerosene lamp he took out paper and pencil and wrote Maggie a letter telling her about the empty gallery and the for rent sign. He didn't seal the envelope because he decided to finish the letter once he knew what had happened to cause Henry Montgomery to announce to him that he had sad news about Chauncey Oliphant.

Zemo rose early, made some coffee but was in no mood for breakfast. Neither was he in any mood to draw. He drank two cups of coffee before loading up and driving to The River Bank. He arrived to watch Montgomery open the front door and step in. Zemo left the pickup parked across the street and walked over to knock on the door. Montgomery opened the door and let Zemo in, locking the door afterward.

"I lock up when I get here early because there's always someone who think he or she needs to talk to me before the bank opens. Anyway, this way we can talk in peace."

They went to Henry's desk and Zemo sat down across from the banker.

"I don't know whether or not you knew that Chauncey Oliphant was a …," Henry began. "He liked men better than women."

"He seemed kind of swishy but he always treated me all right."

"Chauncey treated everyone all right. Anyway, are you aware that he had a partner in Taos?"

"Yes, he sent some of my work there."

"Well, Chauncey's partner in Taos was also Chauncey's lover boy and they would meet as often as possible in Phoenix."

Zemo shrugged. "I don't know much about that sort of stuff," he said.

"I don't either, but I learned a little talking with Chauncey. You see I financed Chauncey's gallery here in Yuma and a friend of mine, another banker in Taos financed their place in Taos. I must say they were always good pay on the interest."

"What is this sad news?" Zemo asked, impatient with Montgomery's rambling.

"Yes, yes. I'm sorry I got to wandering off. Well, Chauncey came in one day and told me that his boy friend in Taos had broken up with him. Seems the Taos boy friend had found another lover boy. I could see that Chauncey was having a terrible time holding back his tears. I don't know anything about two boys breaking up so he told me it was just like a man and a woman breaking up a relationship."

"Is that all the sad news?" Zemo asked.

"I'm afraid not. Chauncey then asked me what the balance on his note was and I told him. He wrote a check for the entire amount on a bank in Connecticut. I gave him his note back and wrote "paid in full" on the face of it. The following day the police answered a report of a gunshot in the vicinity of Chauncey's gallery. The door to the gallery had been left open so they walked in and found Chauncey on the floor with a single gunshot through his mouth, dead.

"My god, that's terrible," Zemo said.

"I'll say it is. The police found the note I had returned, so they came to me to ask if I knew of any relatives he might have had. I was totally shocked at the news. Chauncey had given me the fellow's address and phone number being as how they were partners on the galleries. I gave the name and number to the police and told them I would also contact him."

"What did the boy friend in Taos say?" Zemo asked.

"He was pretty shook up and said he would come down to Yuma and take care of all the stuff under the partnership."

"I reckon from the look of the empty gallery he must have come here."

"He arrived with a truck and cleaned out the gallery. I asked him about Chauncey's personal stuff in the house that he rented. He said that I could give it all to the Salvation Army because Chauncey had no living relatives."

"Did he have much stuff?"

"Not anything with much value, but I guess the Salvation Army can use it."

"That all leaves me wondering what to do. I have a collection of drawings and paintings that Chauncey told me he wanted and now there's no gallery," Zemo said.

"Do you have a contract?"

"No, I worked with Chauncey on his word and mine."

"You said that the boyfriend in Taos liked your work?" Montgomery asked.

"That's what Chauncey told me."

"My advice would be to contact Ben Hungerford in Taos. That's the ex-boyfriend's name."

Henry opened a drawer in his desk and pulled out a file, took out a piece of paper, copied some information on a note pad and handed it to Zemo across the desk. "Get in touch with him and see if you can sell him your collection."

"Thanks, Mister Montgomery. I appreciate your help."

"If there is anything I can help with let me know, Zemo."

"Thank you."

Montgomery saw Zemo to the front door and unlocked it for him. "Let me know what Hungerford says about your collection. In fact, why don't you bring it in here right now so I can call Hungerford and describe what you have."

"I'll be right back, Mister Montgomery," Zemo said as he headed for the pickup and trailer parked across the street.

He grabbed the portfolio case from inside the trailer and carried it back to the bank. Montgomery had waited by the door to let him back in. Back at the desk, Zemo took out the various paintings, pen and inks and pencil drawings to show the banker what he had done.

"These watercolors are magnificent," Montgomery said. " I thought you only worked in pencil and pen and ink."

"I met a girl on a ranch near Rinconada who showed me watercolors."

"She certainly showed you well," the banker said as he went through the collection carefully.

"I had worked in watercolors in school, but she showed me the improvements in the paints."

The banker finished looking at the work and looked up at Zemo. "I am going to call Ben Hungerford right now. I have his home phone as well as the gallery's, but the gallery should be open as they are an hour later in New Mexico."

He picked up the telephone and asked the long distance operator for the number. After a half a minute or so, Montgomery sucked in his breath ready to talk. "Ben Hungerford, this is Henry Montgomery in Yuma. Remember me, the banker?" I have Zemo Doyle with me. He has a magnificent collection of mostly watercolors that Chauncey had ordered and he wants to know if you are interested in the collection... They would be an excellent addition to any gallery...Yes I know you would have to see them...Here. Let me give the phone to Zemo and you both can talk this over."

He handed the ~~phone~~ across the desk to Zemo and Ben and Zemo talked for five minutes. Zemo described the subjects and ended the conversation with, "All right, I'll drive to Taos and see you in a couple of days."

"At least he seems interested," Montgomery said.

"Who knows? He said he liked my other work and that it had sold quite well. He sounds kind of swishy, too."

"Don't worry about the duck, he has a boyfriend who came here with him to help with the driving."

"I hate to sound ignorant, but where is Taos?" Zemos asked.

"You are not ignorant, Zemo. I don't know where Taos is either. The truck those gay boys drove here had New Mexico plates."

Montgomery opened the side drawer in his desk and pulled out a map. "This is a map of Arizona and New Mexico. We ought to be able to find Taos on it," he said, unfolding the road map. "Here's Albuquerque," he said pointing with his finger. "Santa Fe is not far from there. Here's Taos, north of Santa Fe. My, that's quite a long way from here. I have never been to New Mexico."

"I went through it on my way from Missouri to Rinconada to see my uncle, but I never went as far north as even Albuquerque."

"It looks to me like you need to head to Phoenix, then to Globe. From Globe, go through the Salt River Canyon up to Springerville and over to Socorro, New Mexico. From there you just head north until you get to Taos. I am sure glad I don't have to drive that far."

"I guess I'll find a map at a gas station and get going. I told that fellow I would be there in a couple days but it looks to me to be a longer drive than that."

"You are probably right on that score, Zemo. I have never been much for traveling. Yuma has been my home all my life. Anytime I traveled it seemed too cold."

"Well, Mister Montgomery, I sure do appreciate all your help. Some day I will send you a painting."

"That would be nice. Thank you, Zemo, and the best of luck to you."

They shook hands and Zemo left the bank, climbed into the pickup and drove to a gas station where he filled the tank and got a map of Arizona and New Mexico. He arrived in Phoenix at dusk and parked his rig out of town on the road to Globe. The following day, during the grinding trip over the Salt River Canyon, he was afraid the pickup towing the trailer might overheat because of the steep grade going up out of the canyon toward Springerville. The beauty of the canyon and being able to drive down to the Salt River to see the multi-colored cliffs that had been cut over millennia would stay in his mind forever. The idea of returning to paint the canyon made him wish that he were not in such a rush to reach Taos to sell his collection of paintings and drawings.

It was late when he stopped for the night in Socorro. After arriving in Taos in the afternoon of the third day he drove around looking for the Arte Place Gallery. He found it on a side road. He parked in front of the rustic looking building with its hand painted sign beckoning art lovers to view the collections.

He took his portfolio case from the trailer, went up the two steps to the door of the gallery and opened the door. A bell tinkled as he entered and a man came out to meet him.

"Good afternoon. Welcome to Arte Place," the man with curly blond hair said.

"I'm Zemo Doyle coming here from Yuma," Zemo said.

"Oh, yes, yes, we talked on the telephone. I see you have brought your work. Let's have a peek. All right?"

Zemo opened the case and withdrew the paintings carefully, placing them on a long table that sat to one side of the long room, the walls of which were covered with all sorts of paintings.

"Mister Oliphant told me you had good luck selling my work that he sent you," Zemo said.

"As a matter of fact, I did quite well with your work. I see you have expanded to watercolors."

"Yes. I thought Mister Oliphant would be surprised," Zemo said.

"Poor dear Chaunce. What a terrible way to end things."

Ben Hungerford looked at Zemo's work, scratching his chin from time to time and waving his hand and saying, "swell" when he came to a painting he especially liked. When he had finished looking through the pictures he looked at Zemo and squinted his eyes. "Your work is quite good. As you can see I still have some of your previous work from Yuma."

Zemo wandered around looking at the drawings he had done before. He was amazed at the prices Ben was hoping to get for them. Coming back to the table he asked, "I would like to sell what I have. Do you want to buy them?"

"I'll buy all you have for two hundred dollars," Ben said.

"That's less than half what Mister Oliphant paid me," Zemo said with annoyance in his voice.

"Oh, come now, dear boy," Hungerford said. "Chaunce probably had his eye on you."

"I don't think I like what you are saying Mister Hungerford," Zemo said, clenching his fists.

"Now, don't get upset. I went to a great deal of expense going to Yuma for all this stuff that belonged to us."

"It seems to me you did quite well seeing how you only owned half before Mister Oliphant killed himself. And, incidentally, I went to a great deal of expense driving to Taos."

"Look, Mister Doyle, I don't have a clue why dear Chaunce did himself in, but we were partners. The stuff belonged to both of us and I have the paperwork to prove it. I think I would like to have you put your work back in your portfolio case and leave."

"You didn't need to say that because that is exactly what I was going to do on my own. Mister Oliphant was a fine man to deal with. After meeting you I can't understand why he was ever your partner in any way."

Hungerford opened his mouth to say something, but Zemo said, "Hungerford, don't say another word. You are a true coyote bastard."

Zemo lifted his case off the table and went out the door. Back in the pickup he sat there for a few moments seething with anger. "I should have punched his lights out," he said to the steering wheel.

Starting the pickup, he drove to a gas station, filled the tank, and also asked the attendant where a good place to camp might be. The man directed him to the Rio Grande Gorge where there was a place to park and he could also see the deep gorge with the Rio Grande flowing at the bottom.

Having successfully followed the attendant's directions, Zemo stood looking at the scene determined to paint it first with early morning light. While eating supper he decided that after he finished the painting of the gorge he would return to Taos to try to sell his work to one of the other art galleries.

Night still blanketed the land when Zemo got out of bed to make breakfast and wait for sunrise. The sun had not even begun an appearance when he finished breakfast so he wrote a letter to Maggie explaining where he was, why and what had happened after such a long drive. He looked out of the trailer window leaving the envelope unsealed. He saw that first light had eased onto the plateau. Leaving his painting gear in the trailer he walked the twenty yards to the gorge. As he stood there the early morning light began making shadows on the west wall of the gorge.

Zemo stood mesmerized by the changes of beauty. He couldn't even think about his paints, or trying to capture what he looked at. It was all too much for his mind to jump back to painting. An automobile drove up and parked not far from where he was. The people got out and were taking photographs. Their conversation interrupted his state of trance. He hurried back to the trailer and carried his paints and paper out to the edge of the gorge and began working. He worked unmindful of the photographing tourists until the man came over and was looking over his shoulder.

"What are you painting?" the man asked.

Zemo did not look away from the painting. "An elephant," he said.

The man walked back to his car and drove off with his wife in the passenger seat.

As he looked at the gorge and painted, Zemo saw the changes in color and shadows as the morning progressed. He quickly changed to a new sheet of paper to capture the differences. By eight o'clock he had finished except for a few spots that needed touching up. He took the work inside the trailer and did what he thought would improve the paintings.

By the time he had finished he was ready to go gallery hunting in town. Before leaving he turned away from the river toward the East and stood looking at the Sangre de Cristo Mountains capped with snow and marveled at their grand beauty. "I must paint you before I leave for California," he said to the mountains. Packing up everything, he climbed into the pickup, started it and drove back to Taos. Parking the rig on a side street he began strolling around the town looking in gallery windows trying to see what their works looked like because none had opened. He had never seen such a small town that had so many art galleries. Out of the seven that he looked in through their windows, he thought that there were four prospects for his work. As the front doors began opening he returned to the trailer to fetch his portfolio case. He did not include the paintings he had done of the Rio Grande Gorge that morning.

The first gallery he entered had many oil paintings in ornate frames. He had not seen them through the front window. In spite of the collections that did not resemble his work, he asked the owner if he would be interested in watercolor paintings.

"I'll look at them, but we don't handle many watercolors," the man said.

Zemo took his collection out of the case and showed it to the man who raised his eyebrows when he saw the quality of Zemo's work. "You are quite good," he said. "I think you should go show George Kimball at the Brush and Palette Gallery. He is across the street and down a block. George carries mostly watercolors. I just don't have enough wall space for a large inventory."

"Thanks," Zemo said. "I'll give him a try."

He put the collection back in the case and left the gallery, following the directions to The Brush and Palette. He was glad to see the "open" sign and walked in. "Are you George Kimball?"

"That I am," the man said.

"The man at the Taos Gem Gallery told me you might be interested in my work."

"Well, let's have a look," George said.

Zemo took the collection out of the case again and showed the work to the gallery owner. George looked carefully as he rubbed his belly with both hands. Zemo told brief stories about the subjects.

When he finished showing Kimball the paintings he watched the gallery owner go to his desk and sit down, pick up a pencil and do some calculations on a pad of paper. George looked up at Zemo and smiled.

"You do nice work. I like your subjects and I like your composition. You have an excellent sense of color. However, I am almost full of inventory, but summer is not far away. I can give you only eight hundred dollars for the collection."

Zemo had a rush of joy, but scratched his head like he had seen horse traders do. "I did a couple nice paintings this morning out at The Rio Grande Gorge. Let me go get them from my trailer. It is only a couple of blocks away."

"That sounds interesting," George said.

Zemo wanted to run to the trailer but kept a walking pace in case George looked out of his front doorway. Reaching the trailer, he unlocked the door and took the two new paintings from the table where he had left them to dry thoroughly. Walking calmly back to the gallery he walked in and put the Rio Grande Gorge paintings on the table on top of the others.

Kimball looked at them. "These are the best I've seen of the gorge. You must have gotten there early."

"I slept out there," Zemo said.

"How much do you want for these?"

"I haven't thought about a price for them," Zemo said.

"I'll pay you two hundred for both if you'll sign them," George said. "That will be one thousand total."

"That sounds reasonable to me," Zemo said.

"I also want to have first chance at your next collection. Here's my card and you can contact me when you have gotten some more paintings together."

"I will do that, Mister Kimball. Before I leave Taos I must paint the mountains with their snowcapped peaks. I don't know how long that will take once I get started, but as soon as I leave Taos I will be heading to Santa Barbara, California. Would you like some seashore paintings?"

"If they are as good as these, I will be glad to look at them. In fact when you get the Sangres done I would enjoy taking a look at those works."

Zemo signed the paintings then watched as Kimball wrote a check to him for a thousand dollars.

"The bank should be open by now. If you have any problem cashing this check have them telephone me."

"Thank you, Mister Kimball. I will let you know my address as soon as I get one."

Zemo drove to the bank with Kimball's check and had no problem getting his cash. He almost wished he had gone to Ben Hungerford's gallery and shown him the check. Before mailing Maggie's letter, he wrote another paragraph telling her of his good fortune with George Kimball. He also mentioned his plan to paint the mountains around Taos.

Before the day was over Zemo had found a perfect spot to stay while he painted. It was an abandoned field with an old barn quite similar to the Salas barn in Pinnacle, Arizona except the base was made of stone masonry instead of adobe. He parked so that he had an inclusive view of the mountains from the trailer's back window. As he enjoyed his supper he watched the sunset make the snowcapped peaks glisten and turn ruby red in spite of their distance. Relaxed after selling his collection he celebrated with two drinks of tequila from the bottle he had purchased at a small store on the outskirts of Taos.

As darkness invaded and no lights were visible from the barnyard he turned on his kerosene lamp and wrote another letter to Maggie describing the mountains that he planned to paint. The people at the store told him about Rio Hondo as a beautiful stream to paint, especially in this spring season when the runoff from the melting snow made it a wild torrent as it gushed over the rocks and occasional fallen pine trees. It was the longest letter he had written to Maggie.

Zemo felt that he should stay around Taos for a while to take advantage of the extraordinary beauty of the natural landscape before going on to California. He decided he enjoyed the life of a traveling artist far more than that of a traveling rodeo cowboy. As he crawled into bed he looked forward to his attempt to paint the grandeur of the mountains. He slept soundly until shortly after sunrise.

From the trailer he took his paints, a sheet of the new paper that he had purchased in town the same time he had bought a new easel. Setting up facing the Sangre de Cristo Mountains he positioned the easel so that he would always have a clear view of the segment of the mountains he had decided to begin with. Zemo felt exhilarated as he began to paint. Instead of standing in awe as he had at his first glimpse of the Rio Grande Gorge, he began painting with new confidence. It was a feeling of being in control of the work instead of the work being in control of him. By noon he had finished what he considered the preliminary painting to capture the shape and basic essence of the mountain's grandeur. He still contemplated the light as he stood back to critique his work. Thinking that he needed the light of the setting sun to give a more vivid picture of the slopes, he put all the equipment away in the trailer after deciding to unhook the trailer and take a trip into town.

Just as he started to get into the pickup a man drove up in a dilapidated sedan with the door bottoms rusted out. He stopped and slowly got out of the old vehicle and ambled over to where Zemo stood. He was an elderly Mexican man with grooves making canyons all over his face. He wore a hat that was probably as old as his automobile. It had sweat stains half way up the crown and the beaded hatband looked like it was part of the hat. The brim was straight and not curled like many in the Southwest.

"*Hola!*" He said.

Zemo nodded, not knowing the Spanish necessary for a greeting more than *buenos días*.

"This my land," the old man said, guessing that Zemo spoke only English. "Why are you here on my land?"

"I just stopped to paint a picture of the mountains," he said.

"You a painter?"

"Yes," Zemo said.

"How long you stay?"

"I don't know. May I have your permission?"

"I think all right," the old man said. "You have picture?"

"Yes, I'll get it out of the trailer," Zemo said, and went to the trailer and opened the door. He took the painting of the mountain and showed it to the old man.

"Beautiful," the old man said, rubbing his chin. "I been up there when I young cowboy."

"I used to be a cowboy," Zemo said.

"I rode mules up in Los Sangres and took care of wild cattle. Too wild some. We never got those down to brand."

Zemo kept looking at the old man trying to find the words to ask him if he could paint his portrait.

"I am José Ochoa," he said.

"Zemo Doyle, pleased to meet you, José.

"Pleasure is mine," José said.

"I would like to make a picture of you, would you mind?"

"Go ahead. I got nothing to do right now."

Zemo returned to the trailer and got the easel and a clean sheet of paper. He decided to do the portrait in pencil rather than watercolor in order to get done in less time. He could always put color in later.

He asked José to stand next to his car and look toward the mountains. Zemo went to work marveling at the old man's relic of a face that had seen more seasons than Zemo could imagine. The old man's eyes had clouded with age, but Zemo cleared them in his mind so that when he started putting the watercolors down Ochoa's eyes would be brighter to capture his persona better.

After finishing, Zemo offered José a cup of coffee which they enjoyed standing in the shady side of the old barn. They chatted about the lives they had led as cowboys and José said that it was a tough life, especially in the high country where the wild ones were. "We tried to get all those wild *cabrones* that were all that was left of the old Spanish cattle. They went wild with their freedom."

"Were they longhorns?" Zemo asked.

"Their horns were too long sometimes, because when we were chasing them through the pine country their horns slowed them down. That was good for us so we could throw our *reatas* and capture them more easily."

"How did you get them off the mountains?"

"We put hobbles on their front legs so they could not strain and break the rawhide *reatas*. Most of the time it took two cowboys a day, at least, to get one animal down off the mountain. Sometimes we had to work alone. Then that was sometimes a rodeo for sure."

"That sounds more dangerous than being a cowboy these days," Zemo said.

"Cowboys these days don't have any idea what it used to be like," José said, as he gazed off toward the Sangre de Cristos.

The two talked on about the old days and Zemo told the old man about the longhorns that Big Joe Goodman had north of Rinconada.

"It is a joke to me," José said. "We got all the longhorns down from the mountains so the bosses could run their fine bred cattle. Now they are raising longhorns again because of the horns and the hides and not the beef."

"That doesn't make much sense to me either," Zemo said. "Those longhorns we used to drive back to the Quarter Circle V were no wilder than the Y Diamond Herefords."

"Turn any cattle into the mountains and leave them free a few years and when you go to get them they will be wild like deer," José said.

Finished with their coffee they walked back toward the trailer. Zemo put the mugs away and brought the mountain painting out with him and handed it to José. "This is for you, José," Zemo said. "When the clouds cover the mountain you can look at my painting and remember the days when you rode your mules roping wild Spanish cattle."

José took the painting and held it out to look at it again. "*Gracias*, Zemo, you are a good *amigo*. I enjoy talking with you. I am glad you are now a painter and not a cowboy."

"So am I," Zemo said, and noticed small tears form in the eyes of the old mountain cowboy. He wondered how old he was, but did not want to ask.

José carried the painting to his old car, opened the door and placed it carefully on the rear seat. Stepping back to shake Zemo's hand, he said, "Zemo, please stay here as long as you want to."

"Thank you, José. I hope to see more of you so we can talk cattle, horses and mules some more."

"I'll see you in a couple of days, he said, and got into the old car and drove off slowly down the road to town.

Zemo stood where he was for several minutes thinking about the conversation he had had with José Ochoa and the tears Zemo had noticed in the old man's eyes after he had given José the painting of the mountains. Then he climbed into the cab of the pickup, started the motor and drove into Taos to wait for the late afternoon light on the mountains.

Parking the pickup on a side street he ambled toward the plaza where he thought he might discover something to paint at a later date once he had finished painting the various aspects of the Sangre de Cristo Mountains. He sat on a bench facing the main street and looked around. Somehow he couldn't get José out of his mind. He not only wondered how old he was, but where and how he lived at his age.

Suddenly a shiny red Cadillac convertible with its top down driven by a woman in a black cowboy hat matching the car's interior raced by, well above the speed limit. He noted the Texas license plate on the rear bumper. What stood out was the red bandana flapping behind her at the same angle as her tawny brown hair. Both flew in the breeze wind created by the fast moving car with its wing windows opened fully.

Zemo followed her with his eyes and watched as she braked the Cadillac to a screeching stop in front of The Mountain Lodge, slumping slightly down in the seat for a few moments until the bellman came out of the front door of the hotel to take in her luggage. She opened her door, slid out of the seat, stepped to the rear of the car and opened the trunk. The bellman took two large suitcases and a smaller one from the trunk and carried them into the hotel. Zemo watched as the woman walked, hips swinging through the door. A few minutes later he saw the bellman come out of the entrance, get into the Cadillac and drive it to the alley next to the hotel. Zemo had never seen anything like that anywhere he had ever been.

He sat on the bench for twenty minutes looking eastward occasionally to gauge when the mountains would get splashed with the light just before sunset. He had seen it the night before and knew that if he could somehow capture that light on the mountain slopes he would have an exquisite portrait of the mountains. He figured he had a little over an hour to wait before he drove back to the trailer to begin painting. As he looked at the mountains the motion of someone striding toward him distracted his thoughts.

It was the woman who had driven up to The Mountain Lodge in the Cadillac. He turned toward her. She strode with determination straight toward him, stopped short of where he sat on the bench and with her hands clasped behind, her bosom almost spilled from the top of her peasant type blouse, she said. "Hi, cowboy. You shouldn't be sitting here all alone."

Zemo wanted to vault from the bench and run away, but he stayed seated and looked up at her. She tilted her head and looked with an inviting smile that sent Zemo back to his position on the bench without further thought of escape.

I am Sherry Grant from Dallas," she said. "What's your name, cowboy?"

"Zemo Doyle."

"Where are you from?" Sherry asked, and touched his leg just above his knee.

"I don't really know anymore," Zemo said. I just wander around painting."

"Wow, an artist. You look like a cowboy to me."

"Used to be, but I changed my mind," Zemo said.

"I like a man who can change his mind. I changed my mind."

How's that?" Zemo asked, settling down from his initial shock at the forwardness of this Sherry Grant from Dallas.

"I know you saw me drive by in my red Caddie because I caught you watching me through the rear view mirror. That's when I damn near wrecked."

"What does that have to do with changing your mind?"

"I'm getting to that. Just be patient, my dear man. Because I changed my mind, I got that red Caddie and tons of alimony from my ex-husband's oil wells. I've been having lots more fun, and don't have to wait around for him to get home from counting his royalties to have a good time."

"Everyone has to do whatever is needed to be happy," Zemo said.

"Well, now, what do I have here a philosopher or what?"

"I just changed my mind to be an artist instead of a rodeo bronc rider by drawing a man's portrait in a bar in Yuma."

"Speaking of bars how about I buy us a drink over at The Mountain Lodge. They have a great bar that's right off the lobby. You do drink, don't you?"

"Yeah, I drink a little tequila once in a while."

"I can't stand that Mexican crap, but I can probably keep up with my Martinis. Let's go give that bar a try. If the bartender can't make a decent Maritini I would imagine there's another bar somewhere in this burg."

They rose from the bench, and as they walked across the street to The Mountain Lodge, Sherry put her arm around Zemo's waist. He stood six inches taller than Sherry, and, as they made their way to the hotel he reached down and took her hand.

"That's more like it," she said as they reached the door that the bellman opened, flashing his bellman's smile that hoped more for a tip rather than out of genuine friendliness. Zemo glanced back and as soon as they had gone three steps beyond the door the bellman's smile turned into a scowl.

Sherry led Zemo to a table for two by a window through which they could see a patio filled with trees and shrubs that had begun their spring bloom. The bartender came over and asked what they would like to drink.

"Gin Martini, very dry. Whisper vermouth over the glass and not too loudly," Sherry said, borrowing from an old joke.

"And you, Sir?"

"Tequila, straight up," Zemo said.

"Any particular brand?"

"Sauza will be fine," he said.

The bartender returned to his place behind the bar and fixed their drinks. Sherry turned to Zemo. "How long have you been an artist?"

"I started drawing in school but I have only been drawing and painting for money since a few months ago."

"Are you one of the Taos Artists I heard about way down in Dallas?"

"No, I came here to sell a collection and now I am painting the mountains."

The bartender came and put the drinks on the table. "This is mine," Sherry said. "I want it charged to my room. It is number twenty three."

"Very good. Your name?"

"Sherry Grant."

Sherry turned back to Zemo.

"Did you sell the collection?"

"Yes, but not to the gallery I came up here for."

"I don't understand," Sherry said.

"The gallery owner who told me to come here all the way from Yuma, Arizona tried to get the collection for a lousy two hundred bucks. I walked out and told that tightwad in part what I thought of him. I had dealt with his partner in Yuma and he was quite fair with me."

"But you did sell the collection?"

"To a different gallery, and that man wants to have first choice on my next collection."

"How much would you charge to paint my portrait?"

"You have never seen my work."

"All I have to do is look into your eyes and I know I'll like your work, Zemo. I will pay you two hundred dollars."

Zemo raised an eyebrow as he looked at her. "Speaking of painting, I need to go out and check the light at near sunset for a painting of the mountains," Zemo said.

"Do you carry your paints with you everywhere you go?" She asked.

"Just about. If I don't have them, I can't use them," he said.

"All right, go check your light, then get your paints so you can paint my portrait. While you're outside I'll order us another drink."

Zemo went outside, looked at the sky and the mountains, and got

his paints and easel from the pickup. A second shot of Sauza tequila

awaited his return.

"The light outside is about right for a portrait," Zemo said, standing beside the table with his art equipment.

"Lean your things against the wall and finish your drink," she said. "I have a better idea than going outside."

"What's that?" Zemo asked.

"We will do the portrait in my room," she said.

"What's the light like in there?" Zemo asked with an uneasy tone to his voice.

"There's a nice window that I can look out of as you paint."

Zemo sat back down at the table and sipped the tequila. "I think I had better check the light in your room before I set up the easel," he said.

"Don't be silly. I know that the light will be just fine. Besides there's a good sized lamp in the ceiling."

They finished their drinks. Zemo picked up his equipment, and followed Sherry to her room on the ground floor of the hotel. She put the key in the lock, turned it and opened the door. Zemo followed her inside and she closed the door behind them and slid the bolt into its keeper. She went over to the window and opened the shades.

"See, there is plenty of light. I can sit in this chair and gaze out the window. That will make a nice pose."

"You may have something there. Sit in the chair so I can see how the light will be."

Zemo set up the easel and put the paints and brushes on a small table where he could reach them easily. When he lifted his head and turned around he looked wide-eyed with his jaw fully dropped at Sherry Grant sitting in the chair by the window without any clothes on.

"What's the matter, Zemo, haven't you ever painted a nude before?"

"Hell's fire, I have never even seen a naked woman before," he said, still staring at her.

"It's time you did, and I am glad it's me for your first naked lady."

He returned to his paints and began the portrait. He was not sure if he could accomplish the portrait because he had a difficult time concentrating on the work. He wanted to tell her he thought she was beautiful, but decided that he would just enjoy looking at her breasts and the rest of her femininity. He began wondering why her ex-husband had treated her with such carelessness making her wait at home for his late returns. He settled in to the painting and determined to concentrate on the work at hand in spite of the circumstances.

It seemed like he had painted for at least a half hour before he stood back and looked at what he had done thus far. "I like it so far. I just hope I can capture your beauty," he said.

"Let me see it," she said, rising from the chair and walking behind him to see the painting. "I knew you were good. That's really nice."

Zemo leaned over to make a few touch ups on what he had done. Sherry stood behind him, reached around and began unbuttoning his shirt. Zemo felt what she was doing and continued to touch up a few places.

"I'm not finished yet," he said.

"There's plenty of time for that," she said. "I have something else in mind."

Zemo put his brush down and turned to face Sherry. "I've never done it before."

"Wonderful. I can teach you all I know and you will become an expert."

"What do you mean?" he asked.

"If you are as innocent as you say you are, and I believe it, you need to know there is a lot more to making love than just doing it like horses and cows, cowboy. Why not get out of your clothes so I can get you in bed."

Zemo took off his clothes and stood looking at her as she climbed onto the double bed. "What about my painting of the mountain at sunset?"

"Dear Zemo, the mountain will stay where it is and there will be another sunset tomorrow. Come now, it's lesson time."

Evening dusk had fallen before they came out of room twenty-three and went into the dining room for supper. Sherry ordered her usual extra dry Martini and Zemo stuck with his Sauza tequila. While waiting for their drinks they smiled at one another, but did not converse. The waiter brought the drinks and took out his order pad.

"Have you had time to read the menu?" The waiter asked.

"Give us a little more time, please," Sherry said.

The waiter left and Sherry looked over at Zemo. She lifted her long-stemmed Martini glass. "Here's to Lesson Number One, Zemo," she said.

Zemo lifted the shot glass of tequila. "Helluva lesson, that number one," he said.

They ordered supper and satisfied their other appetites. After an arm in arm walk ambling through the village they sat down on a bench in the plaza. "What do you want to do tomorrow?" Sherry asked.

"I have painting to do. Remember your portrait is not quite finished."

"Can you finish it before we go to breakfast?"

"I didn't know we were going to have breakfast together. I'll have to make sure I get up and drive to paint the mountains."

"That is ridiculous, Zemo. You are spending the night with me in Room Twenty-Three."

"Do you mean Lesson Two?"

"There's homework for Lesson One we need to do."

Zemo laughed. "Then let's go to the bar, have a couple more drinks and then do our homework."

"Now you are catching on to the schedule," she said.

Zemo decided to finish the portrait after breakfast. There were just a few touch up spots, mainly on the chair, but he also wanted to make sure he had painted her neckline curves to blend into her shoulders smoothly. When he had finished and signed the painting he washed his brushes, covered his paints and handed the portrait to Sherry.

"There it is," he said. "I hope you like it."

Sherry held it up and looked at her own image, moving her head around as if she tried to appraise the work. "I was right, Zemo. You are damn good at painting, too. Since we got the homework done last night and now I have all my clothes off why don't we start Lesson Two?"

"Sounds fine with me," Zemo said. "I hope I never graduate."

After lunch Sherry followed Zemo to the trailer after he bought a block of ice to put in the icebox to keep the few perishables from spoiling. He parked the pickup as if it was hooked to the trailer and showed Sherry his house on wheels after shoving the block of ice in the icebox. "This is quite small, Zemo, do you ever feel claustrophobic?"

"I don't know what that means," he said.

"Closed in, cramped, feeling unable to escape an enclosed spaceis what it means."

"I don't seem to be bothered by that sort of thing, in fact I find it cozy. However, it was nice to sleep in your bed last night. This bed would be pretty tight quarters I'm afraid."

"We don't have to worry about that because I have Room Twenty-Three."

"You mentioned last night that you like to fish for trout," he said.

"I used to love going out to the Hondo and fish. My ex-husband tried to teach me how to fish with flies but I never could. I just used worms and caught more trout than he did. Of course that angered him. He always had to be a 'big man'. I really got sick of that crap."

"Let's get some fish poles and go fishing," Zemo said. "We can take the pickup and save messing up that red Caddie on the dirt roads."

"I don't mind getting the Caddie dirty, I can get it washed, but if we catch any trout they might stink up the trunk."

"We need a bag of some sort to keep the fish we catch in until we get them home," Zemo said.

"They probably have something like that at the hardware store where they have fishing poles," Sherry said.

They took the truck to town; bought what fishing gear they would need, including a canvas bag that would hold ice to keep the fish cool if they did indeed catch any. The hardware store even sold worms. As Sherry took her wallet from her purse to pay for the purchases she dropped some cards on the floor. Zemo squatted down to retrieve them. One was her Texas driver's license, obvious with the large "Lone Star" logo in the middle. Still down near the floor Zemo glanced at the license and saw that she was forty-two years old. He gathered the fallen cards, stood up and put them on the counter as the clerk counted out her change.

"Thanks, Zemo," she said, and put the cards back in her wallet.

Zemo said nothing about his discovery but found it incredulous that a woman with her body and energy could be more than twice his own age. He raised an eyebrow as he thought that it was no wonder she could teach him all those lessons. She had had enough experience to write a book about it.

The drive to the Hondo took less than forty-five minutes. They parked in a small clearing, readied their equipment and began fishing for trout. Sherry caught the first one that was a foot long and appeared to be a meaty specimen. She also caught the second trout that was the same size.

"You're quite a fisherman," Zemo said.

Sherry put her index finger to her lips because Zemo had shouted his sentiment over the twenty yards between them. The noise of the stream full of snow melt rushing down over the rocks made it close to impossible to hear anything else. Zemo turned toward his line as he felt a nibble on the worm. He waited. When it felt like the fish had taken the bait he gave a slight jerk on the rod and then knew he had something on his line.

Landing the trout on the bank of the stream, he hastened to grab the fish's body and extract the hook from its mouth. The fish measured fourteen inches. Zemo carried his trophy to the bag and put it in. He returned to his rod, baited the hook again and cast it back into the fast moving water just below a windfall that slowed the flow enough so that there was a back eddy, a good place to try for another.

Sherry caught a big one. After extracting the hook, she carried it over to the bag. "How about that one? He's damn near big as a whale," she said.

Zemo smiled, reeled his line out of the stream and went over to the bag containing the fish. Sherry was still there smiling at her accomplishment.

"What are we going to do with all these trout?" he asked.

"I'll give them to the cook at the Inn. Tomorrow there will be a trout special on the menu and I'll bet we get one 'compliments of The Chef'."

"Then let's catch a couple more," Zemo said. " I have never seen so many trout in my life."

"Where in hell have you been? There's enough trout in the Hondo to feed the world."

Zemo watched Sherry fish, catch trout, and land them in a sort of melody to fishing. He wanted to drop his pole and line, grab his paints and easel, and start a series of this woman in a black cowboy hat with round, firm breasts pushing out the upper part of a bright red blouse and catching trout from the Río Hondo in northern New Mexico.

It didn't take but a few minutes for him to trot over to the pickup, grab his art equipment and return to his place on the bank where he had a full view of Sherry working the stream. Rapidly he set up the easel, got the paints and brushes out and captured a cup of water from the stream. Sherry continued fishing pretending to be oblivious of Zemo at his easel.

Zemo caught her in a perfect pose, quickly used his pencils to draw the basic picture before she went to land another fish. Finished with the drawing, he decided to do a series of pencil drawings for a combination of the different positions she struck for the various activities of fishing she went through. The number of fish she caught and thrust into the game bag didn't cross his mind. He just tried to capture the scene that he considered unique. Most fishing pictures he had seen always had a man holding the pole and a big, beautiful trout jumping out of the stream with an artificial fly in its mouth.

He had finished the last pencil drawing when she walked over with her fishing pole over her shoulder. "Zemo, I am totally bushed. The bag is full and now I see you doing art while I am providing dinner."

"I had to draw you fishing, Sherry. This is something a helluva lot different than anyone has drawn. Wait until I do it in watercolor."

He showed her the drawings.

"Wow, do I really look like that when I am fishing?"

"That's the way I see it, Zemo said, and began loading his gear back into the pickup.

When they arrived at the trailer, José Ochoa greeted them from the driver's window of his old car. Zemo stopped the pickup and trotted over to see his friend. Sherry followed at a walk.

"Hey, José, it's good to see you," Zemo said, shaking the old cowboy's hand through the open window of the car.

"I was driving by and saw that red Cadillac car and wondered what was going on," the old cowboy said.

By this time Sherry came up and stood next to Zemo. "I would like you to meet Sherry Grant from Dallas, Texas. The red Cadillac belongs to her."

"A pleasure to meet you, Señorita," Ochoa said. " I was admiring your red car."

"Wanna go for a ride?" Sherry asked.

"Gracias, but no gracias, Señorita. I have ridden too many wild horses in my day."

After thinking of all the trout Sherry had caught, Zemo blurted out, "José, we caught a bunch of fish today, would you like some?"

"Sure, amigo, I can always eat *truchas*."

"What do you mean, *truchas*?"

"I guess you gringos call them 'Trout'," José said.

"We have a full bag," Zemo said, holding up the canvas bag containing the catch.

"Bueno," he said. " I have neighbors who need food."

"Take them all," Zemo said. "Come back soon."

Zemo gave the bag of fish to his new friend and watched him drive away in the old car.

"Who in hell gave you the right to give my fish to that old Mexican?" Sherry asked.

Zemo hesitated a few moments as he watched Ochoa drive out from the Ochoa barnyard. He tried to remember the words that Sherry had used. Once remembering how she had expressed herself Zemo began to wonder about the woman who had so willingly given him lessons about what men and women did for each other's pleasure.

"Sherry, that old Mexican, as you refer to him, is my friend. Before I was born he snaked wild cattle out of the mountains that I want to paint. That old man is of the land. He harbors a wisdom that is long gone. Remember this is 1947. José Ochoa is eighty years old and still wants to know what is going on in the world. Do you?"

"Of course I do," she said. "Let's not get into some long drawn out discussion about philosophy, my ex could do that for hours on end even after I had fallen asleep waiting for him to take me to bed. By the time he finished and I had come awake he was no longer in the mood."

"Where do you want to fish tomorrow?" Zemo asked, dropping the previous conversation.

"I know a spot on the Rio Grande and another stream down by Dixon that always has fish willing to get caught. Leave the stuff here and we can drive into town in the Caddie and come back in the morning for the fishing gear. Put the worms in your ice box."

Leaving the pickup and trailer at the barn didn't bother Zemo except he wanted some time alone to paint the sunset. "Why don't I follow you in later after I get done painting the sunset?"

"No, Zemo. Come along now. It's time for another lesson,"

Zemo locked the trailer and pickup after putting the worms in the icebox and the poles inside the trailer. Seeing Maggie's letter on the counter he suddenly thought about her and stood experiencing a terrible feeling of guilt.

The feeling eased and he got in the Caddie for the ride to the hotel. They had two drinks in the bar before going to Room Twenty Three for the "lesson". Zemo felt the remnants of his guilty conscience about cheating on Maggie but was able to rationalize that Maggie and he were not engaged and not even pledged to "going steady". He enjoyed the "lesson" and after supper he enjoyed the drinks and another "lesson" from the woman who seemed insatiable.

Ever since he discovered how old Sherry was he had had a strange feeling that she was using him in several ways. He had little experience with women, especially those twice his age and that left him wondering about what he was doing in the arms of Sherry Grant from Dallas. He wondered if she had any children and if so, how old were they? Again he thought about Maggie and felt another pang of guilt about what he was doing with Sherry.

After breakfast the following morning Sherry and Zemo drove the Caddie to the trailer where Zemo retrieved the fishing rods and worms.

"Are there enough worms?" she asked when he got into the pickup for the drive to Sherry's fishing hole on the Embudo Creek.

"Here's the can," he said. "Poke around and see how many are left. We can stop at the hardware store if we need more."

Zemo started the pickup and steered it out of the barnyard. As they approached the plaza Sherry said, "Zemo, I think we should buy more worms. The current can get rough on Embudo Creek at Dixon. Sometimes the streamflow grabs the worms off the hooks before the trout get their chance."

At the hardware store they bought more worms and Sherry went over and grabbed another canvas bag. "Since you gave that other bag to your Mexican friend we will need another," she said. "Best we get some ice for it."

Zemo almost told her she could well afford another canvas bag but held his tongue. He had grown weary of her petulance. They returned to the pickup and drove out of Taos toward Sherry's choice of a fishing place.

There was a turnout where Zemo parked. Taking the fish poles and worms they went down a narrow path to the river. They stood on a small peninsula of boulders that jutted out into the river. Sherry baited her hook and began casting the worm downstream into the eddy behind the boulders. The worm hadn't been in the water a minute before she hooked a nice rainbow measuring sixteen inches. She landed the fish easily and shoved it into the new canvas bag. Zemo watched. He did not bait his hook. What distracted him was the sight of the Río Grande flowing with lots of snowmelt coming from the mountains, rushing on its way to the Gulf of Mexico. What he saw and felt was the power of the water as it rushed to its destination. Zemo decided that he needed to paint that power, but he would wait until he could be alone to capture the scene without having to do as he was told by his so called teacher.

Sherry caught another but tossed it back because it didn't compare with the first catch of the day. She kept the third fish and looked around to see Zemo looking at the river. "Aren't you going to fish?" she asked.

"Maybe," Zemo said. "I just like watching the river."

"Harumph," she grunted. "Damned artists don't know a good fishing hole when it is right in front of them."

Zemo looked upstream without replying.

When Sherry had put five good-sized trout into the canvas bag she stood looking at Zemo who was still mesmerized by the river. "We might as well drive down to Dixon while there's still room in the bag for more fish, or are you tired of fishing?"

"I am having a great time just watching this river," Zemo said, and picked up his fishing rod that had not been used to cast since the day before. He grabbed the canvas bag and began the ascent to the pickup.

Embudo Creek was well named. In English, Embudo means funnel. Zemo parked and they walked over to look at the torrent of water rushing in an almost rage as it headed for the Rio Grande.

"How do you like this spot? Sherry asked.

"It's beautiful," Zemo said without taking his eyes from the creek. "I must come here sometime and paint this."

"Well, I'm going to fish it," Sherry said, taking her rod and the worms to the point where the highway engineers had diverted the creek and made a place where the raging current missed and a tranquil pool had evolved. Zemo followed without his fishing rod. All he wanted to do was look at the multitude of views and scenes to catalogue in his mind as places that deserved painting.

Sherry filled the canvas bag with the trout she caught from the pool. Zemo carried the bag up to the pickup. Sherry loaded her pole and put the worms in the bag with the fish. They drove north, back to Taos. When they were near the hotel Sherry said, "Zemo, if you will stop in front of the hotel, I will take the fish in to the kitchen before you give them all away again."

He braked the pickup to a stop at the hotel entrance and waited as Sherry got out of the cab, reached into the back for the fish and carried the canvas bag through the door that the bellman had opened for her. She came back shortly and climbed back into the cab. "We'll have a free trout supper tonight," she said.

Zemo put the pickup in gear and drove out to the barnyard without saying another word. All he thought about was painting the mountains at sunset. Pulling in to the barnyard he spotted José sitting on a mule in the shade of the old barn. He waved at his friend and José waved in return.

"Your Mexican friend won't get any fish today," Sherry said.

Zemo did not reply. He got out of the pickup, took his easel, paints and paper and walked toward José. "Stay right there," Zemo said. "You are in a perfect pose for a painting."

Sherry stood next to the Caddie. "I thought we were going to the hotel," she called out.

Zemo stopped and turned around to face her. "Not now," he said. "I need to paint José on his mule and then I am going out to paint the mountains at sunset."

Sherry stomped around the Caddie, opened the door with a yank and plopped herself into the black leather driver's seat. She turned on the ignition, slammed the shift downward and pushed the accelerator to the floor. The Cadillac leaped toward the gate throwing sand at the pickup. Without slowing she turned onto the road and sped away to town.

"*Muy bronca la mujer,*" José said.

"What does that mean in English?" Zemo asked.

"Very wild woman."

"Yes, she can give a wild ride," Zemo said.

"I would rather lope my mule."

"What's your mule's name?"

"His name is Alfonso."

The mule put his ears forward.

Zemo set up his easel and went to work on the painting.

As he painted he and José chatted about cattle, horses and mules. At one point José asked why Sherry had driven off in such a hurry.

"She doesn't like not getting her own way," Zemo said.

"There are children like that," José said.

"Think about what a spoiled brat she must have been," Zemo said.

"Once in a while you come across a horse or mule that is the same way. Some people say mules are stubborn, but I have news for those people. Mules are just smart."

"I heard my uncle say that once. He told me you can turn a horse into a grain bin and the horse will eat and eat until it founders and its hooves swell up. But you put a mule in the same grain bin and the mule will eat only as much as it needs and then stops eating. Is that right?"

"Your uncle must know both horses and mules because he is *correcto*."

Finishing the painting, Zemo took it into the trailer, put it on the table to dry and went back to José. "I am going to the other side of town to paint the mountains at sunset," he said.

"I came out here to show you my Alfonso but also to invite you to have breakfast with me tomorrow."

"That would be great," Zemo said. "After watching that *mujer bronca* race out of here, I won't be going to the hotel tonight."

José dismounted, took a stick in his fingers and smoothed out the sand with his other hand. He drew a map in the sand so that Zemo could find his house in the morning.

"That sounds simple enough," Zemo said. "What time?"

"Anytime you get there. I will cook you huevos rancheros and I will bet my *Seguro Sociál* that you will like them."

"What the hell is *Seguro Sociál*, José?"

"Social Security."

"I will see you as soon as I get there," Zemo said.

"*Muy bién, amigo.*" José said, and booted Alfonso out of the barnyard.

Zemo put all his painting things into the pickup, making sure he took plenty of paper. By the time he started down the road for the other side of town José and Alfonso had disappeared. As he entered Taos he saw the red Cadillac convertible heading toward him. There was Sherry driving hell bent with a man with curly black hair and sunglasses in the passenger seat looking at her as she spoke to him. Zemo was careful to keep well over to the right hand side of the road to avoid any possible collision with the *mujer bronca*.

He breathed easier when he saw the red Caddie in the rear view mirror. "Another student," he said to the pickup's steering wheel. Zemo stopped across from the hotel entrance. He got out of the pickup, grabbed the fishing rods and headed for the entrance door where he met the bellman. "Can I help you?" The bellman asked.

"Yes, I think you can," Zemo replied. "Please give these fishing poles to Missus Grant when she returns."

"I would be happy to," the bellman said.

"Thanks," Zemo said, without reaching into his pocket.

He reached the spot where he wanted to stand to paint the mountains at sunset. As he set up the easel he thought about Maggie. In spite of knowing that Sherry was history, he still felt pangs of guilt even though he and Maggie had never spoken any agreement to "go steady". Then he began thinking about the question:

how can two people "go steady" when one is in California and the other is in New Mexico?" He still felt guilt having taken "lessons" from Sherry Grant.

It was nearing sunset time. Zemo stood in front of the mountains watching every change in color. He had drawn a faint outline in pencil so that he had a base to work from because at sunset the color changes quickly, but not the shapes of the mountains. He began to think that it might take several evenings to capture the scene he thought so beautiful. However, he also had noticed that the sunsets seemed to be different every evening. He felt glad that he would no longer have to conform to Sherry's schedule.

A white billowing cloud hovered above the mountains. As the sun sank the cloud shone in a rosy glow before the color struck the slopes. Zemo stood with brush in hand waiting. The color changed and he began to mix his paints when the mountain took on a brilliant orangey red. The snowcap glistened. He worked rapidly capturing the sunset on the mountains before dusk changed to darkness.

Arriving at the trailer after dark Zemo felt relieved that he was not in the hotel with Sherry. He stretched out on the bed, closed his eyes and the next thing he knew the sun was sending early morning light through the window. Remembering that he was to have breakfast with José he straightened things up inside the trailer and made sure he had his art equipment in the pickup.

Following José's directions he found the small adobe house in a few minutes, not far from the place he had been staying. He parked the pickup and stepped out, taking his mountain painting with him to show his friend. José came outside to greet him. "*Buenos dias, amigo*," he said.

"Good morning to you, José," Zemo said. "I brought my sunset painting of the mountains to show you.

Zemo held it up for José to look. "That is beautiful," the old cowboy said. "I have seen that color on the mountain all my life. That is why the Spaniards named the mountains "Sangre de Cristo". That means Blood of Christ. I will bet you can sell this painting for good money."

"I hope so. I am trying to get enough money together for my trip to California. This morning I will visit the gallery to which I sold my last collection and see if the man wants what I have done around here."

"What happened to *la mujer bronca*?"

"Who knows? I saw her with a new boyfriend as I was going to paint the sunset."

Zemo put the painting back in his portfolio into the pickup and then returned to the house. They went in and José showed him around his home and some old photographs of José and his friends all mounted on horses or mules. "That was the entire crew of the Rancho Cebadilla one Fall before we rode out to gather." José pointed to one of the riders. "That was me when I had twenty-four years."

The huevos rancheros were filling. Zemo liked the chile salsa and the generous amount of cheese. The two talked about ranching and José told him all about his family's long journey from Mexico and how some had suffered wounds during the Pueblo Indian Rebellion against the Spaniards.

Zemo knew he would not see José again before he left Taos so they said their goodbyes. "When you get back here don't forget to stay at my barn," José said.

"I will. Take good care of Alfonso."

Zemo felt somewhat sad to be leaving his newfound friend, but he needed to get to California to see Maggie before she graduated. She had written that she had been offered a job as a courtroom artist so she wouldn't be going back to Rinconada.

Before hooking the pickup to the trailer Zemo took the paintings he had finished and sold them to George Kimball at the Brush and Palette Gallery. George paid him more per painting than he had before. Zemo swelled with pride as he walked back to the pickup, went to the bank to cash the check and drove back to the trailer. He had everything ready to start south to Albuquerque. There he planned to take Highway 66 clear to Los Angeles before turning north to Santa Barbara. After hooking up the trailer to the pickup he left José's barnyard and drove through town. As he approached the side road to Dixon he raised his eyebrows when he saw the red Cadillac parked above Embudo Creek. He had thought about stopping there to paint, but the sight of the familiar automobile caused him to snicker and stay on the highway.

Passing through Santa Fe he thought it was strange that such a small city was the capital of the state. He filled his gas tank in Albuquerque before finding a place near Highway 66 close to the bridge over the Río Grande to spend the night. The sound of the flowing river coming through the open window lulled him to sleep.

By late morning the following day he reached Gallup near the Arizona border. As he drove through the town Zemo decided that most of the population was Indian. He found it an interesting place to look at but he wanted to continue to Flagstaff, stopping only for gas. Long before he arrived in Flagstaff he saw a tall mountain far in the distance. The nearer he came the taller the mountain seemed. At the outskirts of the town he pulled over to consult his map. The San Francisco Peaks were what he had been watching. He thought about stopping for a day to paint, and after seeing a log building with a sign on its front announcing "The Museum Club", he pulled in to the parking area and went into the most interesting bar he had ever seen. When his eyes adjusted he saw all sorts of relics on the walls from cattle and sheep working tools to Indian beadwork and weapons.

He sat down on a rawhide-covered barstool and enjoyed two tequilas before asking the bartender where a good spot might be to park his trailer and paint a picture of the mountain. The man with a large, bushy mustache directed him to go through town and park in a wide-open park like area called Fort Valley. "From there you will get a nice view of The Peaks. Just beyond, there is a dirt road that leads to Hart Prairie, but you should probably unhook from your trailer to go over that one."

"Is that road worth the trouble?' Zemo asked.

"Damn right. When you reach Hart Prairie you can see both Humphrey and Agassiz Peaks. Humphrey is the highest point in the state. It stands twelve thousand six hundred and forty-three feet high."

"Sounds like I need to go there," Zemo said.

He downed another shot of tequila, left the bar and drove to Fort Valley where he found ample room to park the trailer. After supper he wrote a letter to Maggie explaining how far he had gone and how he was looking forward to seeing her in Santa Barbara. Before going to bed he thought about Sherry and wondered how long he would feel guilty about that affair.

The following morning he unhooked the trailer and drove the pickup out to the highway. The first dirt road had a small sign indicating that it went to Hart Prairie. He turned right and followed the two-rutted road that wound its way upward from the valley. Passing through a large grove of aspen fresh with their spring green leaves almost half way out, he came to a corral. Someone had carved the name "Espil" on one of the planks that held woven wire fencing. Zemo knew by the woven-wire fence that whoever Espil was, he raised sheep. He continued a short way to find the road opening onto a large, treeless prairie. He stopped the pickup and got out to look at the mountain and the highest point in the state.

He saw large aspen groves in a mosaic with spruce on the steep slopes of the mountain. Without traveling further he set up his easel and paints to begin a portrait of The San Francisco Peaks. The top of Humphrey and Agassiz Peaks had small snowcaps that Zemo liked as a contrast with the azure blue sky. When he had finished, he decided to explore the prairie until sunset for another painting of the Peaks with sunset colors decorating them.

Hiking up the prairie he came upon a reservoir with salt blocks held up by old rusted pipes. As he went to the water's edge he could see the multitude sheep hoof prints in the muddy ground. Hearing noises coming from the grove of pine near the waterhole, Zemo glanced up to see a man in a green uniform riding a bay horse toward him. As the rider got closer, Zemo saw that he was wearing the uniform of a forest ranger but his hat looked more like his own Stetson.

"Hello there," the rider said. "Have you seen a band of sheep around here?"

"I sure haven't," Zemo replied. "There are lots of tracks in the mud."

The ranger rode to the water's edge and looked down. Turning toward Zemo he reined the bay around and dismounted leading the horse around the reservoir a short way before approaching Zemo again. "I guess I missed them," the ranger said. "I was supposed to get a count from the herders. Because I grew up in Nogales on the Mexican border I'm the only one who speaks Spanish so I get any job that means talking with the herders. They are all from Spain and don't speak any English."

Zemo shrugged. "When do they generally come in to water?"

"It depends on how far away they bedded down for the night," the ranger said. "I'm Brian Barlow, and work for the Coconino National Forest."

"Zemo Doyle, I am painting the mountain."

"She's a beauty, all right, and sacred to the Hopi and Navajo," Barlow said. "Is that your pickup down by the road?"

"Yeah. I am waiting for sunset to try for the color."

"You have a while to wait, Zemo," Barlow said.

"That's all right, I am having a good time walking around," Zemo said. "Incidentally I noticed ash beneath the green growth here on the prairie. Was there a range fire recently?"

"There's a fire every fall here. The sheep men burn the prairie claiming it is good for it. I agree with them, but the rest of the rangers disagree. They put out every fire they can spot from their towers."

"Why don't they put out the range fires here?"

"They can't get to it before they have burned up to the aspen groves."

"Why do you disagree with the rest of the rangers?"

"It's kind of a long story," Barlow said. "I have a degree in range ecology from the university where I studied under Robert Humphrey. He is a pioneer in fire ecology."

"I have never heard of all that," Zemo said.

"Ecology is the study of organisms in relation to their environment and to each other. Humphrey says we have neglected the role of fire in maintaining prairies and grasslands. He also says that the mesquite invasion of the desert grassland is the result of fire control."

"I worked on a ranch near Rinconada that was getting too much mesquite and catclaw."

"Without periodic fire all that range down there will become a forest of brush," Barlow said.

"Suppose the forest service won't let the sheep men burn this prairie?" Zemo asked.

"At this elevation I would expect ponderosa pine to invade the prairie," Barlow said.

"What happens when you tell the forest service what you have learned about fire from that fellow Humphrey?" Zemo asked.

"I don't say anything about my knowledge of fire because I want to keep my job. Someday I hope there will be a chance to voice those theories without jeopardizing my job."

"I guess I am too independent to worry about some job if I can't say what I believe in."

"To each his own," Barlow said.

"Do these sheep spend the winters here?" Zemo asked.

"Heavens no, there is far too much snow here on the Peaks and it gets damn cold. The sheep men drive the bands down to the Salt River Valley farms in the fall and then back up here in the spring once the prairie has gotten a start. There's a trail that comes up Black Canyon. That seasonal trail driving back and forth is called "transhumance" and it takes place in many parts of the world."

"Wow, I guess there's lots you can learn in college," Zemo said.

"You don't have to go to college to learn a lot of good stuff," Barlow said.

"I learned a lot about cows from my uncle."

"Another interesting thing is that the sheep trail is a legal right of way and the cattle ranchers have to maintain gates wide enough to let the sheep get through all the way from here to Phoenix. The herders are all Basque. The sheep men from Phoenix hire them from Spain, and pay all their transportation to Phoenix."

"Why is that necessary?" Zemo asked.

"There is nobody in this country who will spend all that time on a mountain taking care of a bunch of "woolies"."

"That makes sense. I sure wouldn't want that job on a bet," Zemo said.

"If you drive up the road to about where that small aspen grove is and look up at Humphrey Peak just below tree-line there's a bunch of boulders. When the sun is right you can see some shiny metal. That is a World War II bomber that crashed up there."

"Is it worth climbing up to see?" Zemo asked.

"It's nothing but scrap metal, but if you get that far you might as well go to the saddle between Humphrey and Agassiz. From there you can look down into the Inner Basin, the crater from the old volcano that made the mountain."

"What's in the crater?" Zemo asked.

"You could spend a month walking around there and still see new things. There was a fire in the Inner Basin in the 1890's and there are spruce snags still standing. There are small spruce and bristle cone pine starting to establish themselves. You might consider driving up the road to Locket Meadow and then hike into the Inner Basin. There is a lot to paint in there. Go back through Flagstaff and head toward Tuba City. Just when you reach the pass there is a stand of tall ponderosa pine and a road to the left. Take it to Locket Meadow. There's a sheep water hole there, too."

"That sounds like a worthwhile climb," Zemo said. "I have enjoyed talking with you, Brian. I wish you well and hope you find the sheep. I need to get myself ready for sunset. Maybe the sheep will come to water and I can paint them."

Barlow mounted the bay, reined him back to the trail he had taken and disappeared into the forest. Zemo descended from the reservoir and returned to the pickup. Following the ranger's advice he drove as far as the small aspen grove that surrounded a small dry stream that was covered with grasses.

He got out of the pickup and looked up at the mountain where Barlow had described. The sun was perfect, shining on the metal so that Zemo located the crashed bomber. Right then he decided that he would get going early in the morning, drive out to the prairie again and climb Humphrey Peak. He also liked the new angle better for his sunset painting.

While he waited for sunset Zemo painted the aspen grove adding water to the stream. The prairie served as a background. Finishing he took out a new sheet of paper and penciled in the mountain's profile and noted where tree line was and two obvious rockslides. When the sunset bathed the slopes he began painting. He was disappointed that the color was not as spectacular as on the Sangre de Cristo Mountains in New Mexico. However, it was worth the trip.

Before he returned to his trailer it was dark enough to require turning on his headlights of the pickup. As he approached the trailer he saw four sets of yellow eyes staring at him. Then the bodies of four deer showed up in the light beams. He stopped the pickup and watched the animals lift their heads to try and catch scent. They stayed looking at him as if mesmerized until one of the group turned and walked into the darkness. The remaining three followed shortly afterward. Zemo pulled up to the trailer and parked.

The following morning he drove out of Fort Valley before sunrise, eager to get to Hart Prairie to climb the sacred mountain and look into its Inner Basin. Parking the pickup next to the aspen grove again, he set out in early morning light heading for the summit of Mount Humphrey. Having been a cowboy, Zemo had never been one to like hiking long distances without the benefit of a horse, and he had never climbed a mountain in his life. By the time he reached the large aspen grove that bordered the prairie he was ready to sit down and rest. After he recovered his breath at the high elevation, he entered the grove and trudged his way upward winding through the trees. He wished he had asked the ranger if there was some sort of trail to follow up the mountain. At one point he heard a noise and glanced in that direction to catch a glimpse of three elk rumps charging through the trees.

At last he came out of the grove and found an almost pure stand of pine trees with shorter needles than the ponderosa. He assumed that they were bristlecone pine that the ranger had mentioned. Once he had passed through that stand of trees he could see that he had almost conquered the mountain. As he climbed the last part he looked to his left and saw the crumpled wreckage of the bomber. Still climbing he reached the site of the crash and saw the pieces of aluminum complete with rivets. He could barely identify what might be fuselage or wings. Scrap metal is what the ranger had said. He continued his climb to the saddle.

Once there he looked back down the slope and saw his pickup looking tiny. He also looked at the vast plateau and saw other mountains less tall than the one he had just climbed. He turned, took a few steps and looked down into the Inner Basin. "Wow," he said aloud. "What a place that is. Tomorrow I am going to go there."

He saw springs giving forth water. He saw a stand of tall trees at the base of Mount Agassiz and all the snags still standing from a fire that almost cleaned out the basin of all its trees in the 1890's. He saw another smaller mountain at the end of the Inner Basin and then beyond, another. To the north he saw an array of volcanic cones and an area of mesas. He could see why people called them tablelands. Shifting his eyes eastward he saw what looked like a waterfall on a river. To the south Mount Agassiz blocked out the view of the city of Flagstaff, but he saw what looked like a primitive road leading from the saddle between Agassiz and Mount Doyle over to the saddle he was sitting on. The road appeared to have been covered by a large rockslide at one point. He remembered the name of Mount Doyle from the map he had bought from a rack in the Museum Club. Zemo sat down and just looked.

He remembered what Barlow had said about it being a sacred mountain to the Hopi and Navajo and could understand why, because of its grandeur and beauty. Zemo had never been much for religion but he could feel an aura of sacredness about the mountain in his own thoughts. His eyes digested the beauty, and he was glad he had not tried to carry all his painting equipment. After the climb he now knew that he would still be trying to reach the saddle. He might have given up. Hiking is not for cowboys.

Zemo was in no hurry to leave the top of the mountain. Instead of returning to the pickup over the same route he had taken, he decided to cross over to Agassiz Peak on the saddle, and descend on that other slope to see what might be different. He was not disappointed. There was a trail that led downward. He wasn't sure what kind of a trail it was, but he followed it through another stand of bristlecone pine with a few stunted scattered spruce near timberline. Below that the spruce grew taller and he could recognize game trails that he followed downward. Just above the reservoir where he had met Ranger Barlow he saw a two-rut road that led to a clearing. He ignored that and headed downward at an angle to where he saw the pickup waiting for him at the bottom of the aspen grove, not far from the west end of the prairie.

Once seated in the pickup he took off his work shoes and sat there contemplating his day on the mountain before returning to the trailer. There was enough daylight left so that he decided to drive to the mature ponderosa pine stand on the west side of the highway that signaled where the road to Locket Meadow was. He hooked up the trailer and began his relocation. It seemed like Flagstaff slept early as he drove through the town. The Museum Club tempted him to pull in for a couple of shots of tequila but he resisted that beckoning sign and continued to the spot the ranger had described.

The grove of ponderosa pine was open with a vigorous looking stand of grasses between the tall reddish barked trees. Zemo drove almost to a cinder cone that formed the north border of the pine forest and parked. He unhooked the trailer to prepare for an early start in the morning. Before going to bed he wrote a letter to Maggie telling her about his mountain climb and the Inner Basin he had seen from the saddle between the two peaks. As he addressed the envelope he realized that the mountain climb had tired him more than he had thought. He gave up the idea of painting the view of the Inner Basin he had seen from the saddle and went to bed.

Zemo awakened to early morning light, scrambled some eggs and fried some bacon as he gathered his paints, brushes and paper along with the easel to stow in the pickup for the drive to Locket Meadow and what had looked like a long walk up through the basin. Just before sunrise he started the pickup and drove up the narrow two-track road that had been cut into a steep hillside before it reached the more level ground near the meadow. Driving around the last bend in the road he saw Locket Meadow surrounded by tall, old aspen, some with peoples' names carved in their trunks. Near the entrance there was a pond fed by a stream coming from the basin. He saw the same kind of salt blocks as were at the reservoir on Hart Prairie. Another sheep waterhole, he guessed.

Just as he parked under a tall pine sheep began arriving on a trail that entered the meadow from the east. He sat in the cab and watched. Two dogs kept the flock moving. A herder carrying a long pole with a leg hook on one end followed them in and sat on a boulder while the sheep crowded around the edge of the pond to drink their fill. The herder pulled out a sack of Bull Durham tobacco, rolled a cigarette and smoked it as he waited. Zemo waved.

Zemo took a small sheet of paper and drew the scene with a pencil as a preliminary to a later watercolor. He made notes about the contrast between the slightly yellowish gray wool and black faces to the green grass in the meadow. That finished, he took his equipment and followed the trail leading to the Inner Basin, waving again to the herder sitting on the boulder on his way out.

He had had nearly a bird's eye view of the basin from the saddle between Humphrey and Agassiz peaks so he knew what route he wanted to take once he arrived on the trail from Lockett Meadow. Staying to the southern end of the basin he came upon a lot of spruce snags from the 1890's burn. They stood like sentinels watching over the new growth of spruce and bristlecone pine started after so many years. A large aspen grove occupied what looked like a raised platform of ground about in the middle of the basin. He walked around the eastern end of the grove and came upon a generous spring from which gushed a stream of icy cold water. He stopped, knelt and with cupped hands scooped some of the pure water to drink. "No wonder the Indians regard this mountain sacred," he said

At the base of Agassiz Peak there was a pure stand of tall spruce that had obviously escaped the 1890's fire. The trees grew close together. Above them on the slope the trees were stunted until above tree line vegetation was limited to flowers and a few grasses.

Consulting the map he saw the road that he had seen from the saddle the day before was marked "Weatherford Road". It went up the outside of the mountain from Schultz Pass over Doyle Saddle and around Fremont Peak where it switch backed up the basin slope of Mount Agassiz to the saddle he had sat on. Below the road and Doyle Saddle he noticed a rusted auto hulk that was so old and rusty that Zemo had no idea of its age. He wondered if the Doyle whose name went to one of the Peaks might be related to him.

Feeling he was in some sort of paradise, Zemo wandered around the Inner Basin until mid-afternoon painting three scenes before making his way back to Lockett Meadow to drive back down to where he had left the trailer. After touching up the paintings he decided that he liked the one of the spruce snags the best. Stowing them in his portfolio he cooked supper and drove to town to mail Maggie's letter and to stop at The Museum Club for a couple of tequilas after his second day of exploring on the sacred mountain.

Before leaving the spot beneath the tall ponderosa he finished painting the sheep drinking at pond's edge in Lockett Meadow. The Painting also showed the dogs waiting next to the sheepherder who was sitting on the boulder smoking a cigarette.

He hooked up the trailer, drove back through town and westward toward Williams. To visit The Grand Canyon crossed his mind, but he felt that it was out of his way, and he was getting anxious to see Maggie in California. Feeling the desert heat now that he was down from the plateau, he recalled the high temperatures around Rinconada. Taking off the felt Stetson, he put it on the passenger seat. The air coming through the window cooled his head for a few moments as the sweat evaporated. At Needles, across the Colorado River, he thought about his days in Yuma with the Quechan Indians. He decided to rest in the shade of a large grove of trees along the river, and continue across the Mojave Desert at night to escape the blistering heat of the day.

The air cooled slightly after sunset but it was still hot. Zemo had been able to sleep for a while in the afternoon, and started the pickup for the drive across the desert that would bring him closer and closer to Maggie. By morning he had reached Victorville. There he turned off Highway 66 onto a small road that his map told him would lead to Ventura. He wanted to see the Pacific Ocean as soon as possible.

After his trip across the desert the Ventura ocean front the next morning struck Zemo as a different world with the ocean breezes cooling him off. He parked the truck and walked on the beach looking at the Pacific Ocean. Zemo was glad that the morning was young enough that the beach had few people and that they were mostly walkers. When he returned to the pickup and trailer he made a breakfast of bacon and eggs. As he ate he thought about Maggie and wondered what the beach at Santa Barbara was like.

Back on Highway 101 he headed north to his destination, hardly noticing the beautiful coastline. As he approached Santa Barbara he found a place to pull off the highway so that he could reread Maggie's letter telling him how to find her. He opened it. She gave him directions to the guesthouse she had rented to the rear of the house at 110 Juniper Street. It seemed simple enough to find as long as he could find the main street and drive away from the ocean. Pulling back on the highway he followed the signs and turned on the street she had told him about. Going through the center of Santa Barbara he passed the Presidio, the largest building in view. Continuing up a grade he looked at each street sign until he saw Juniper and turned right onto it, heart pounding.

A short distance later he saw 110 painted on the curb in front of a house that looked the same as the one next door. He parked his rig, and walked along a path to the side of the house leading to the guesthouse to the rear.

Suddenly the door to the guesthouse burst open and Maggie came running toward him. "Zemo," she said, and stopped in front of him as he held out his arms for her. Zemo bent slightly, wrapped his arms tightly around her and kissed her.

"Damn, but it's good to see you, Maggie."

"I was looking out the window wondering when you would get here," she said. "Then, there you were, walking up the path."

"Let me look at you," he said, and took her face in his hands and kissed her again.

"Come on in and I'll show you where I have been living the past two years," she said as they walked back to her house.

"When do you graduate?" Zemo asked.

"I told you in my last letter. Maybe you didn't get it."

"There wasn't anything at general delivery in Flagstaff."

"I graduated last night," she said, and opened the door. "You didn't miss anything."

Maggie led the way into the guesthouse. "It is pretty small, but the rent was what I could afford."

"Hey it's twice as big as my trailer."

Zemo glanced around at the place that was essentially one room with a bathroom and small kitchen area. The bed folded up against the far wall.

"Do you have to pull the bed down every night?"

"Yes, but it is easy," she said.

Zemo started having one of his feelings of guilt from having had his affair with Sherry. He sat down at the small kitchen table.

"How about some lunch? Are you hungry?"

"I'm not hungry yet," he said.

"Is something wrong? You sound like you are bothered."

"I suppose I am bothered. I hope you will forgive me," he said.

"Forgive you for what, Zemo?"

"I guess I need to tell you and be ready to accept whatever I have to accept. I met a woman in Taos who was old enough to be my mother."

"That's no big deal," Maggie replied.

"But, I went to bed with her, and afterward I felt guilty as hell."

"Why did you feel guilty?"

"Because I love you, Maggie and I shouldn't have done what I did with that woman."

"I think that is absolutely wonderful," she said, and smiled.

"Why in the world would you say that? I thought you would be angry."

"I think I would be disappointed if you didn't feel guilty, but because you did I know for sure that you love me."

"Hmm,"

"Another thing I just thought of. If this woman was old enough to be your mother she probably taught you a lot about all that stuff that I know nothing about. The only thing I have ever seen was cows and horses doing it. Now you can show me all about it."

Zemo stood up from the chair, took Maggie into his arms and looked at her for a few moments. "You are a wonderful woman, Maggie. Can we get married in Santa Barbara today?"

END